$10,000 IN SMALL, UNMARKED PUZZLES

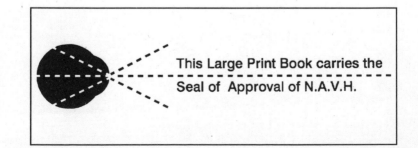

This Large Print Book carries the Seal of Approval of N.A.V.H.

A PUZZLE LADY MYSTERY

$10,000 IN SMALL, UNMARKED PUZZLES

PARNELL HALL

THORNDIKE PRESS
A part of Gale, Cengage Learning

GALE
CENGAGE Learning®

Detroit • New York • San Francisco • New Haven, Conn • Waterville, Maine • London

LIBRARY OF CONGRESS CATALOGING-IN-PUBLICATION DATA

Hall, Parnell.
    $10,000 in small, unmarked puzzles : a puzzle lady mystery / by Parnell Hall. — Large print ed.
        p. cm. — (Thorndike Press large print mystery)
    ISBN-13: 978-1-4104-4728-9 (hardcover)
    ISBN-10: 1-4104-4728-6 (hardcover)
    1. Large type books. 2. Felton, Cora (Fictitious character)—Fiction.
3. Crossword puzzle makers—Fiction. 4. Women detectives—Fiction.
I. Title.
PS3558.A37327A617 2012
813'.54—dc23   2012000814

Published in 2012 by arrangement with St. Martin, LLC.

Printed in the United States of America
1 2 3 4 5 6 7 16 15 14 13 12

For Bill,
thanks for the memory

NEW SHOOTER

I want to thank Fred Piscop, for constructing the crossword puzzles used in the blackmail notes in this book. For his first time out, Fred was pretty impressive, deftly incorporating the blackmailer's cryptic clues. One would have thought Fred had been blackmailing people all his life.

I want to thank *New York Times* crossword puzzle editor Will Shortz, for recommending Fred, and for constructing the Sudoku puzzles which, in conjunction with the crosswords, convey the blackmailer's demands.

As always, I would like to thank American Crossword Puzzle Tournament champion Ellen Ripstein for editing the puzzles and saving me from my own folly, at least in that regard.

CHAPTER 1

"Just keep calm," Cora said as she piloted the Toyota around the curve.

"Keep calm?" Sherry said from the backseat. "You're the one driving like a maniac."

"Don't distract her," Aaron said. He had his arm around Sherry and was squeezing her hand.

"Distract her from what?" Sherry said. "Skidding off the road?"

"Hold on," Cora said. "I'll get you there."

Cora was driving Sherry to the hospital. Sherry had just gone into labor, which seemed to panic the expectant great-aunt more than it did the expectant mother. Cora had fallen all over herself bustling Sherry into the car. Aaron had been lucky not to be left behind.

The expectant parents were headed for the new hospital, a two-story structure of stone and steel built in 1970. The old hospital had closed in 1984, so there was only a six-year span during which Baker-haven had two hospitals. Nonetheless, the residents still referred to the hospital by the mall as the new hospital.

"How are the contractions?" Cora asked.

"Wonderful," Sherry said. "I have a deep, abiding love for all of you. Do you have any more dumb questions?"

"I'll think of some. Aaron, did you bring her something to bite on?"

"Bite on?"

"Like in the movies when they're digging out the bullet without anesthesia."

"I'm fine," Sherry said. "Cora. I need you to focus. The Puzzle Lady column."

"What about it?"

"You have to turn in the puzzles so people think you write the damn thing."

"They're not going to be impressed if I turn them in wrong."

"It's not a problem. I'm your secretary. I send out the crossword puzzles you create. I'm on maternity leave, so you have to send them out yourself. You're somewhat spooked by the technology. You hope you get everything right."

"You can say that again."

"No, I don't mean it. That's the part you're playing. It's your excuse for any problem with the puzzles that you can't deal with. Anything you have to ask me about. Any technical, secretarial problem having to do with the functions of the computer programs. You're the genius who scrawls crossword puzzles on the backs of napkins. I'm the functionary who deciphers your handwriting and prints the things out."

"Couldn't have said it better myself. Could I actually hire a functionary while you're in the hospital?"

"No."

"Why not?"

"Because I write the puzzles. Because you couldn't construct one if your life depended on it."

"That's cruel and hurtful. I'll put that down to labor pains. You're clearly delirious."

"Will you watch the road?"

"I'm watching the road. It hasn't moved since I've been on it."

"You just missed the turn for the hospital."

"Huh?"

"Come on, Cora. I'm not the first person in the world to have a baby."

"Yeah, well, you're early," Cora said.

The baby was premature. Sherry going into labor had caught everyone off guard.

"Five weeks," Sherry said. "That's nothing these days."

"Easy for you to say. They'll knock you out with drugs; you won't feel a thing. They won't even give me a valium."

Cora hung a U-turn, headed back the other way.

The telephone rang.

"Is that your phone?" Sherry said.

"If it is, I'm not answering," Aaron said. "No, not mine."

"Well, it's not mine," Cora said. "I don't have one."

It continued to ring.

"You wanna look in my bag?" Sherry said.

"You don't have to answer," Aaron told her.

"Yeah, but I can if I want to, right? I mean, having a baby doesn't cut you off from the world." Sherry snapped open the phone. "Hello . . . oh, hi, Becky . . . yeah, Cora's here. She can't talk, she's driving . . . yeah, she's driving me to the hospital. . . . No, nothing's wrong, I'm just having a baby. . . . Thank you, but I haven't had it yet. I'm not sure of the protocol, but I think you're supposed to wait until there's an actual infant. So, what do you want with Cora? . . . No, she's driving. You tell me, I'll relay the message . . . You're in trouble and you need her help." Sherry looked up from the cell phone. "Becky's in trouble and she needs your help."

"Tell her I'm busy," Cora said.

"She'll be right there," Sherry said, and hung up.

Cora's mouth fell open. "Didn't you hear me? I said no."

Sherry scrunched on the edge of her seat. "Cora Felton. If you let my having a baby make you give up the things you love, you'll end up hating me and the baby. A sharp, young attorney at law wants your help. You're not going to blow her off just so you can run around the hospital driving everybody crazy. Aaron and I can handle the baby thing just fine. You drop us off, and go help Becky Baldwin." Sherry looked out the window. "Assuming you ever *get* us to the hospital."

"Huh?"

"You just missed the turn again."

CHAPTER 2

Becky Baldwin, easily Bakerhaven's lawyer most likely to be mistaken for a Miss America finalist, had a law office down a side street over a pizza parlor.

"Garlic and eggplant," Cora said, sniffing the air. "Wanna put a side bet on it?"

Becky pushed the long blond hair out of her eyes. "What do you mean blowing me off like that?"

"Like what?"

"One thing you should know about cell phones. If you talk loudly next to a cell phone, the person on the other end can hear. 'Tell her I'm busy.' Now, is that what you tell a person who has an emergency?"

"You're a lawyer. You don't have emergencies. It's not like you're a doctor with a dying patient. If you don't bail out your client, tough rocks, he sits in jail. What's an hour or two? Probably do him good."

"My client's not in jail."

"Then it's not an emergency."

"Yes it is."

"Is it a kidnapping?"

"No."

"Is someone's life at stake?"

"Not really."

"You wanna play twenty questions, or you wanna tell me what it is? If it was really an emergency, I wouldn't think you had this much time to waste."

"Actually, I do."

Cora stood up. "I'm going back to the hospital."

"No, wait. My client's in trouble. They need you to get them out."

"They? You have more than one client?"

"Not necessarily."

Cora suggested practices for Becky which probably would have kept her out of law school and might have even gotten her committed.

"Nice talk," Becky said. "I said *they* to avoid a gender-specific pronoun. I have a client. The client needs your help. It's serious and it's urgent."

"What is it?"

Becky sighed. "It's blackmail."

Cora searched in her floppy drawstring purse, pulled out her cigarettes.

"You can't smoke in here."

"Then let's go out there."

"I don't wanna go out there."

"I don't wanna be here at all."

"Fine. We'll go out there."

Cora and Becky went out of the office and down the steps into the side alley. The odor of pepperoni was almost overwhelming.

Cora lit a cigarette, took a deep drag, exhaled. "Okay, let's talk turkey. If you don't want me to know if your client's a man or a woman, you're not going to tell me who your client is. Which seriously decreases my interest in the matter. Plus the fact that blackmail's illegal, so whatever you want me to do is probably illegal. This is a very unappealing prospect indeed. Start talking. You've got two minutes or until I finish this cigarette, whichever comes first."

"I got a blackmail demand. For ten thousand dollars."

"In small, unmarked bills?"

"Isn't it always? My client wants to pay it."

"What do you want?"

"I want your help."

"In talking your client out of it?"

"No. In making the payment."

"Oh."

"Well, I can't let my client do it. And I'm not going to do it."

16

"I, on the other hand, am expendable."

"Don't be silly. This is right up your alley."

"Oh?"

"It's a mystery. It's intrigue. You're being hired as a private investigator to do something new. You've never been involved in a blackmail, have you?"

"For good reason. People involved in blackmail get arrested. They go to jail. If you don't believe me, ask Chief Harper."

"I'd prefer to leave him out of this."

"I'll bet you would. The whole thing sounds fishy as hell." Her eyes narrowed. "Tell me this isn't something you and Sherry hatched up to keep me out of the hospital. Some secret signal she could text-message you, or whatever the hell it is people do now. Whenever you got it you were to call Sherry on her cell phone, tell her it's an emergency and you had to see me at once."

"You know how paranoid you sound?"

"Hey, when people are out to get you, you're not paranoid. You're either conspiring with Sherry to keep me from the birth of her baby, or trying to involve me in a blackmail. Either way, you're out to get me."

"I'm not out to get you. I'm on your side. I want you on my side."

17

"Making a blackmail payment."

"Unfortunately, that's my side. Are you in or out?"

Cora shook her head. "You'll have to give me more than that."

"Okay, come back inside, I'll show you the note."

"There's a note?"

"Of course there's a note. You can't have a blackmail without a note."

"You didn't mention a note."

"I was leading up to it."

"Spit it out, will you? First you say there's no time, then you pussyfoot around like we've got all the time in the world."

"Actually, we have until noon. That's when you're delivering the money."

"Delivering it to who?"

"I have no idea."

"You're doing it again."

"Sorry, but I have no idea. Come back inside, I'll show you the note."

They went back into Becky's office. She opened her desk drawer, took out a manila envelope. She reached in, pulled out a sheet of paper. It was a piece of white posterboard. Pasted onto it were words cut from newspaper headlines.

PLACE $10,000 IN SMALL, UNMARKED BILLS IN A MANILA ENVELOPE. CLOSED

SERVICE STATION DUMPSTER.

"Well, that's a little ambiguous," Cora said. "But it's gotta mean closed station, not closed Dumpster. Tell Chief Harper to stake out the abandoned Chevron station north of town and pick up whoever comes for the money."

"Yes, wouldn't that be nice," Becky said. "But then my client's good name would get smeared."

"Your client's got something she's willing to pay ten grand for, her good reputation ain't worth squat anyway."

"The actions of my client, whoever he or she may be, are not necessarily motivated by logic. It's a blackmail demand; my client wants to pay up. Whaddya say?"

"What blackmail demand? I see a request for money. I don't see a blackmail demand. I don't see any threat like: If you don't do what I say I'm going to send your wife that motel registration receipt. Or I'm going to prove you forged hubby's will. Or I'm going to tell the authorities where they can put their hands on the arsenic you fed Grandma."

"Nice fishing expedition."

"You can't just walk up and ask someone for money. You've gotta have a motivation. Otherwise, people would be blackmailing

19

each other all the time. So, can we assume this wasn't the only letter? Or can we assume there was something else in the letter?"

"Actually, there was something in the letter," Becky said.

"Oh? What was that?"

Becky reached in her desk, pulled out a sheet of paper, passed it over.

It was a sudoku.

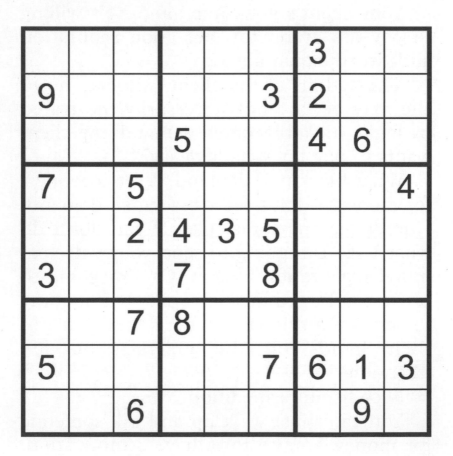

CHAPTER 3

"Sherry put you up to this?"

"No."

"This is legit?"

"Yes."

"You have a client who wants me to make a blackmail payment at noon today?"

"Right."

"And the client specifically wanted me?"

"No. The blackmailer specifically wanted you."

"You're deducing that because of the sudoku?"

"Can you solve it?"

"Of course I can solve it."

"You can't solve crossword puzzles."

"That's different. There are words involved. There's an infinite number of possibilities. With numbers there's only one answer."

"So solve it."

Cora took out a pencil, whizzed through the sudoku.

6	7	8	1	2	4	3	5	9
9	5	4	6	7	3	2	8	1
2	1	3	5	8	9	4	6	7
7	6	5	9	1	2	8	3	4
8	9	2	4	3	5	1	7	6
3	4	1	7	6	8	9	2	5
1	3	7	8	9	6	5	4	2
5	8	9	2	4	7	6	1	3
4	2	6	3	5	1	7	9	8

Becky took the sudoku, looked it over. "Yup. You're the one the blackmailer wanted."

Cora frowned. "What do you mean?"

"Like Cinderella. The glass slipper fits on your foot, so you're the princess."

Cora suggested ways Becky could use a glass slipper that had nothing to do with her feet.

"It's perfectly simple," Becky said. "The blackmailer wants the money delivered by someone who can solve the sudoku."

Cora stared at her. "How the hell do you figure that?"

"The blackmail note."

"It says nothing of the kind in the blackmail note."

"Not that blackmail note."

"There's another blackmail note?"

"Yes."

"One you haven't shown me?"

"Have you seen another blackmail note?"

"Becky."

"There's another blackmail note. I can't show it to you."

"Why not?"

"Because the client doesn't want me to."

"Why not?"

"It divulges matters he or she would prefer not known."

"It's really annoying to keep saying *he* or *she*. Can't you pick a gender and go with it?"

"Sorry."

"This blackmail note that you won't let me see — the blackmailer says they want me to make the drop?"

"No. Just that they want someone in particular, and we'll be able to tell from the next message."

"And the next message is the one I read?"

"Yes."

"So you *are* deducing just from the sudoku."

"I'm deducing from being told I would be able to deduce. The sudoku is the only clue. Who do you think it points to? The Sudoku Lady? The blackmailer wants you. My client wants you. I want you."

"It's nice to be wanted. It would be nicer to know why."

"Because you're an expert in these matters."

"It's my first blackmail."

"You know what I mean. Matters of discretion and tiptoeing around the law."

"Poppycock," Cora said. "There's no discretion involved. I take the blackmail money and leave it in a Dumpster. How difficult can it be?"

"I don't know. I've never delivered blackmail money."

"Is it in a briefcase?"

"No."

"How come?"

"Maybe a half a million. This is a piddling ten thousand." Becky opened her desk drawer, took out a manila envelope that had been folded and taped into a small, rectangular package.

Cora frowned. "That's it?"

"That's it."

"That's ten thousand dollars?"

"Yes."

"In small, unmarked bills?"

"It's in ten packets of twenties. Fifty to a packet."

"Are you sure? If this is a gag it could be paper cut in the size of twenty dollar bills."

"No, it's real."

"Mind if I verify that?"

"Only if you're taking the case."

"What?"

"If you're not, it's none of your business. I'm sure my client wouldn't want me showing it to an outsider."

"Well, I'm not taking the case unless you can prove it's money."

"I can prove it's money."

"Go ahead and prove it."

"Not till you take the case."

Cora scowled. "Are you trying to piss me off?"

Becky smiled. "No, but it's an added perk."

"Show me the money."

"Take the case."

"Show me the money first."

"You drive a hard bargain," Becky said. "All right, I'll show you the money first. On one condition."

"What's that?"

"If it's ten thousand dollars, you'll take the case."

"That's the same thing," Cora protested.

"I can tell you six reasons why it isn't."

"I'm sure you could. All right," Cora said. "How about this? I'll agree to take the case on one condition."

"What's that?" Becky said.

"That there's ten thousand dollars in that package."

"How's that different from what I said," Becky wanted to know.

"It's *entirely* different."

"How's that?"

"I said it."

CHAPTER 4

The abandoned service station was a mile and a half out of town on the southwest corner of North Street and Maple. Cora drove by from every conceivable direction. She saw nothing. Not that she expected to. Still, it occurred to her the blackmailer might be keeping an eye on the station. In which case her driving by so much might be pissing him off. Cora certainly hoped so. She wasn't the least bit happy with the situation, and wanted the blackmailer to feel so, too.

Cora checked her watch. Five minutes to twelve. Would the blackmailer mind if she was early? You wouldn't think so. But some blackmailers were pretty persnickety. At least the ones in the books she read. Granted, they were fiction. Even so, if Cora was going to do the job, she wanted to do it right. And it wasn't just a sense of pride. She didn't want the blackmailer, Becky, or

the mysterious client pointing the finger at her.

Not to mention the police.

Cora shivered at the thought. And was instantly angry. She'd often played fast and loose with the police. But always on her own terms. That was why it didn't bother her. She was always in charge. But here she was, playing by someone else's rules in a game she knew nothing about.

What bothered her most was that she'd let Becky talk her into it. That was not the type of relationship she wanted to have with the young attorney. Cora had worked with Becky before, but Cora had always been in charge, always called the shots. It was never the other way around. And it was important to keep it that way, if they were going to be working together.

Cora frowned. Was that what was happening? With Sherry slipping into the role of wife and mother, was Becky emerging as the heir apparent, the coconspirator, confidant, and aider and abettor? She'd certainly slipped into that role when Sherry was in Kenya on her honeymoon. And with Sherry in the hospital —

Hospital.

She should call the hospital. Cora wished for once she had a cell phone. Not only couldn't she call the hospital, but no one could reach her if something was wrong. Not that anything would be wrong. But still . . .

Aw, hell.

Twelve o'clock.

Cora needed a cigarette.

The hell she did. It's twelve o'clock. High noon. Quit stalling. Just do it.

Cora pulled into the station, drove by the pumps. They were locked. Had been for years, ever since the station closed. It struck Cora as funny. Two large, heavy-duty padlocks protecting the empty pumps. If they were indeed empty. Or was there still gasoline down there? And if there was, would it be possible to tap it? With fuel prices so high, you wouldn't think it would be. . . .

Cora shook her head angrily. She couldn't concentrate. Her mind was leaping with lightning speed from one topic to another. Anything other than the task.

Cora drove on by the front of the station, the plate-glass windows boarded up with chain-mail gates, and around to the side where the air hose was. She wondered if that still worked. Her tires did seem a little flat and —

In the far corner, nestled up against the side of the station, was the Dumpster. Cora had wondered why it was still there. The gas pumps and the air hose were fixtures, but a Dumpster could be picked up and carted away. It was easy to see why no one wanted it. The metal was so badly rusted it was hard to tell it had once been green. The seams were cracked and there were holes in the sides.

A hell of a place to leave a blackmail payment.

Cora walked up to the Dumpster. It was about shoulder height, and had a metal cover. There was a hole for a padlock, but of course there was none. Too bad. If there had been, she could have scrubbed the mission and it wouldn't have been her fault.

Cora raised the lid.

She dropped it with a clang they must have heard all the way to Bakerhaven.

There was a dead body in the Dumpster.

CHAPTER 5

Cora steeled herself, raised the lid again.

The man was about thirty-five to forty. He had brown hair and blue eyes. He was not a bad looking man. Cora would have considered him marriage material except for the bullet in his head.

The man had been shot in the temple. It was recent enough that blood was still flowing. It dripped down, staining the white shirt that he wore with his gray suit and blue tie. He was lying on his back staring up at the sky. Or the lid of the Dumpster when it was closed.

The corner of a folded piece of paper was protruding from inside the front of his jacket, making a little white triangle on his blue tie. Cora pulled it out, unfolded it.

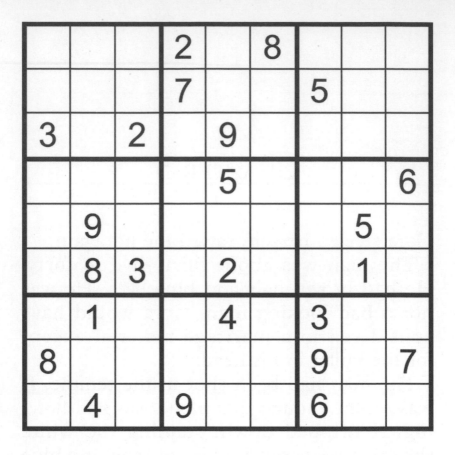

It was a sudoku. That was a stroke of luck. Cora couldn't solve a crossword puzzle if you gave her the answers, but she was a whiz at sudoku. If the police wanted it solved she'd have no problem.

At least with the puzzle.

Cora refolded it, stuck it back in his jacket pocket.

All right, what to do?

She had to get to a phone and call the police.

Except . . .

What was she doing there, and why did she look in the Dumpster?

Good questions. And ones she could not answer. Well, she'd tap-danced her way out of tighter spots than that.

No, she hadn't. It was a question that had no answer. Why did you look in the Dumpster? There was no conceivable reason. She had something she wanted to throw away? So naturally she drove a mile outside of town to an abandoned filling station on the off chance it still had a Dumpster, and lo and behold, it did. Cora could imagine Chief Harper going for that.

No, the anonymous tip. That was what the situation called for. Get the hell out of there. Find a pay phone. Disguise her voice. Report the body. And hightail it home and be there waiting when Chief Harper called her to solve the sudoku.

Cora closed the lid.

Should she wipe off her fingerprints? Absolutely not. That would be obstructing justice.

On the other hand, it would be hard to maintain the position that she hadn't looked in the Dumpster with her fingerprints on the lid.

Cora plunged her hand into her floppy

drawstring purse, pulled out a handkerchief, polished her prints off the lid of the Dumpster.

Okay.

Now go.

There came the sound of a siren. It grew rapidly louder.

Too late.

The police were there.

Hell!

Now what?

She'd have to stand firm and not talk. They couldn't do anything to her. She'd invoke her right to remain silent, and call her lawyer. Then Becky would —

Damn!

The blackmail money!

They'd arrest her and book her and find the blackmail money. How the hell would she ever explain that?

Cora raced back to the gas pumps. The panel on the front of the nearest pump was slightly loose. Cora bent down, pulled at it. The metal bowed outward. When released, it would snap back.

Cora pulled the manila envelope out of her drawstring purse, thrust it toward the opening in the gas pump.

It wouldn't fit.

Cora cursed, pulled harder at the metal plate.

It bowed farther, farther, farther. Just a little bit more.

And it bent!

A diagonal crease across the corner. A good six inches long. There was no way it would snap in place. Well, nothing she could do about that now. Cora bent the corner up. Thrust the package in. Let go.

The corner wouldn't stay down.

Cora banged on it, to no avail. It jutted out at an angle. It practically screamed to be noticed.

Cora reached her hand in behind the plate. She pushed from the outside, bent the metal back over her fist. Not perfect, but it would have to do.

Cora released the flap, stepped back, and was standing calmly lighting a cigarette just as the police car came screeching up.

CHAPTER 6

Chief Harper got out of the cruiser, eyed Cora Felton suspiciously. "What are you doing here?"

"Waiting for you," Cora said brightly.

"Why?"

"You're the chief of police."

Harper scowled. "I know I'm the chief of police. Why are you waiting for me here?"

"You always show up at crime scenes."

"This is a crime scene?"

"Isn't it?"

"I'm asking you."

"Yes, but it seems you already know. You come driving up with your siren blaring, there's gotta be a reason."

Chief Harper took a breath, tried to control his blood pressure. He knew better than to spar with Cora Felton. "Did you look at the body?"

"What body?"

"The one that makes this a crime scene."

"It's a murder, Chief? This being a service station, I was thinking more along the lines of a convenience store robbery."

"Sure," Harper said. "Someone tried to rob an *abandoned* filling station."

"Some crooks aren't that bright."

"Yeah."

Harper turned on his heel, walked around the corner of the station to the Dumpster. He took a handkerchief from his pocket, used it to lift the lid, and peered in.

After a moment he closed the lid gently, and walked back to Cora.

"Did you know that was there?"

"The Dumpster? Of course I knew it was there. I can see it from here."

"Don't play games with me, Cora. Do you know what's in the Dumpster?"

Cora shrugged. "Most Dumpsters contain trash."

"I'm not talking about most Dumpsters. I'm talking about this Dumpster. Did you know, specifically, what was in this Dumpster?"

Cora was saved from having to answer by the arrival of Sam Brogan. The cranky officer drove his cruiser right up to where they were standing, clambered out of the driver's seat, and assumed a put-upon pose. "It's my day off, Chief. What's so all-fired important?"

"There's a corpse in the Dumpster. Set up the crime scene ribbon before people get wind of it."

Sam popped his gum. "Anyone I know?"

"It's no one I know," Harper said. "I can't vouch for your circle of acquaintances."

"I suppose I should have a look."

Sam wandered off in the direction of the Dumpster.

"Now then," Harper said. "You were telling me what brought you here."

"My trusty Toyota. I know there's bad press and recalls and the gas pedal might stick. Still, I like the old girl."

"You ever seen the corpse before?"

"You want me to take a look?"

"Haven't you already looked?"

Cora smiled. "Was that a veiled question, Chief? You didn't used to be so indirect."

Barney Nathan drove up. The medical examiner, as usual, wore a red bow tie. Cora had never seen him without one. She wondered if he wore them to bed.

"Where's the dead man?" Barney said.

"In the Dumpster."

"You wanna take him out of the Dumpster? I'm not climbing in there."

"Soon as we get some photographs."

"What's stopping you?"

"Dan's got the camera."

To a New Yorker like Cora, the idea that a police investigation would be held up while they located the one officer with a camera was somewhat mind-blowing, but the doctor seemed to take it as a matter of course. "You reach him?"

"He's on his way."

While the chief was occupied, Cora seized the opportunity to stroll off in the direction of her car.

"Hey," Harper said. "Where do you think you're going?"

"Sherry's in the hospital. She's having a baby."

"You're not. You can stick around."

"It's her first kid, and it's five weeks premature. I want to call."

"You'll get your chance. We happen to have this murder."

"Seriously. I gotta go."

"Then tell me about the body."

"There's nothing to tell. I'll take a look if you want, but if you don't know him, it's a good bet I don't know him."

Harper nodded. "Loquacious."

"Huh?"

"That's one of your fancy words. When you're it, something's up. I got bad news for you, Cora. You're not leaving here until you answer a few questions in simple, declarative sentences."

Harper went back to look at the body.

Cora glanced casually at the pump. Gas was a dollar sixty-nine. That was something. It was hard to believe the station had been closed that long. The last sale was for twenty-one dollars and forty-two cents.

Farther down the pump a metal panel stuck out. Cora sucked in her breath, tried to tell herself it wasn't that bad. Not like someone had pried it up to hide something. More like something had dented it. A car bumper. A baseball. Though no one would be throwing a baseball at a gas pump, and it wouldn't make a crease. But there was really nothing out of the ordinary. Nothing to draw one's attention to it.

Except her staring at it.

"Hey."

Cora looked up guiltily to see Sam Brogan holding a crime scene ribbon. "What's up, Sam?"

The laconic officer, never one to exert himself unduly, indicated the gas pump with his chin. "That's a gas pump."

Cora caught her breath. "So?"

"Shouldn't be smoking around a gas pump."

She exhaled in relief, shook her head. "Sam, this station hasn't been used in twenty years."

"Even so. Bad habit to get into."

Sam found an electrical cable on the side of the station to tie off to, and began stringing the crime scene ribbon.

Barney Nathan, waiting impatiently for Dan Finley to show up and photograph the body, found himself face to face with Cora Felton. The doctor acknowledged her somewhat stiffly. In the past Cora had occasionally alluded to the fact he might have botched an autopsy or missed a cause of death or two. "What are you doing here?"

"You know, that's just what Chief Harper said. A case of great minds running in the same direction."

"You mean he didn't call you?"

"Why, did he call you?"

"Of course he called me. I'm the medical examiner."

"And yet you don't want to climb into a Dumpster," Cora observed. "Some defense attorney is going to have fun with that."

"What?"

"When it comes to determining the time of death. A defense attorney could probably make a big deal about not examining the body as soon as it was found."

41

Barney Nathan's jaw tightened. He seemed to be looking for the appropriate comeback. Instead, he turned and stomped off in the direction of the Dumpster. Cora could see him conferring with Chief Harper. She smiled as the doctor dragged an old apple crate over to the Dumpster and climbed in.

Harper walked over and joined Cora. "I suppose I have you to thank for Barney's change of heart?"

"I don't know what you're talking about."

"Well, don't think it gets you off the hook. You're not leaving here until you make a full statement."

"In that case, could you do me a favor?"

"What's that?"

"Call my lawyer."

CHAPTER 7

Becky Baldwin screeched her car to a stop behind Sam Brogan's, got out, and strode over to where Cora stood next to Chief Harper. "So, what's the score?"

"Well," Cora said, "there seems to have been a murder."

"Did you do it?"

"No."

"Then I don't see what's the problem."

"The problem is she isn't talking," Chief Harper said.

"Then why is she here?"

"She was here when I got here."

"She was here before you?"

"Yes."

"That must be a little embarrassing."

"Now, see here —"

Becky put up her hand. "Chief. You know and I know Cora had nothing to do with this. If she isn't talking she must have a reason. So, for the benefit of all concerned, why don't you let us have a little talk, as a courtesy, a friendly thing to do. Otherwise I'll demand it as a right, and things will get sticky."

"Fine. Talk to her. I want to know why she was here. Find out and tell me."

"That isn't the way it works, Chief, and you know it. I'll have a talk with my client and we'll see what we can do."

Becky dragged Cora out of earshot.

"So," Becky said. "What the hell happened?"

"You know as much as I do. I opened the Dumpster, found the body."

"Who is he?"

"I have no idea."

"What's your impression?"

"If he was alive, I'd like to date him. Dead, I'd probably pass."

"You think he's our blackmailer?"

"If he is, your client probably did it."

"Nonsense. My clients are never guilty. So, what did you tell Harper?"

"Nothing."

"You didn't tell him you found the body?"

"Of course not. Then he'd know I looked in the Dumpster."

"He knows it anyway."

"How?"

"He knows you phoned it in."

"I didn't phone it in."

"I know. You did it anonymously."

"No, I didn't."

"You didn't?"

"No."

"Then who did?"

"The way I see it, either your client or the blackmailer. If the dead man's the blackmailer, then it's probably your client. Which would tend to piss me off, because that would mean your client set me up to be caught by the cops. It would also mean your client was the killer, so you'd have your own problems. On the other hand, if the dead man is your client . . . You should probably take a look and see if he is."

"Right," Becky said dryly. "If I look, it confirms my client's a man. On the other hand, if I don't look, it confirms it's a woman. So I have to look in either case."

"I don't care what you do, Becky, but the ball's in your court. Chief Harper wants me to talk. You don't want me to talk. I don't want to talk. What's your plan of action?"

"You probably shouldn't talk."

"On what grounds? The grounds you don't want me to probably isn't going to fly."

"An answer could incriminate you, but I hate to admit it."

"*You* hate to admit it."

"I do. But I don't see any recourse. If you tell him what you were doing here, it would incriminate you in a crime. It's a textbook case for invoking the fifth amendment."

"How are we going to explain that?"

"We're not. That's the beauty of the fifth amendment. You're not required to divulge information that would incriminate you in a crime."

"Yes, I understand that," Cora said impatiently. "Legally, technically, we don't have to say a damn thing. Practically, that's Chief Harper, and we have to live in this town. What do we tell him?"

"You wanna go to jail?"

"Not especially."

"Then we can't tell him anything."

"Fine. Then we don't tell him. When Chief Harper asks, I'm not talking on advice of counsel. And when I do that, will he arrest me?"

"Good point. In case you're arrested and booked, why don't you slip me the cash."

Cora grimaced. "That's the other bad news."

"Huh?"

Cora told Becky about hiding the money in the gas pump.

"Good lord. What were you thinking?"

"The same thing you were. If I was arrested, I didn't want the cops finding the blackmail money."

"I don't think that's the best way to refer to it."

"I see no reason to refer to it at all. Particularly since I don't happen to have it."

Chief Harper came walking up. "Okay, ladies. You've had time to straighten out whatever technicality was making you tongue-tied. So, tell me. What were you doing here?"

Cora took a breath. "I refuse to answer on the grounds that an answer might tend to incriminate me."

CHAPTER 8

Chief Harper opened the cell door and let Cora out. He had heard the expression "madder than a wet hen," but never really knew what it meant. He still wasn't sure, but he figured Cora probably qualified, both from the look on her face, and the stream of expletives with which she assessed his performance as a police officer.

"Now, see here," Harper said. "You can't play fast and loose with the law."

"I invoked my constitutional privilege. Which I have every right to do. You incarcerated me for it. Which you have no right to do. That's false arrest. As your attorney will doubtless instruct you."

"*My* attorney?"

"Of course, your attorney. Haven't you ever been sued before?"

"You're suing me?"

"Well, I'm not baking you a cake."

"You don't have the authority."

"Neither do you."

"Yes, I do. I'm the chief of police."

"You don't have the grounds. That's the bone of contention here. You arrested me without grounds."

"I have grounds. You're withholding evidence."

"What evidence?"

Harper hesitated.

"See? You don't even know. My attorney is going to make mincemeat out of your attorney."

"I don't have an attorney."

"Better get one."

Harper ushered Cora into his office.

Becky Baldwin was waiting. "You okay?" she asked Cora.

"She isn't happy," Harper told her.

"What a surprise. How about it, Cora? What did they use? Third degree? Rubber hose? Anything that would up the damages?"

"Now, see here," Harper said. "You're not suing me and I'm not arresting you. We're all friends here."

"Friends don't arrest friends," Cora said. "So, who's the dead man?"

"No one knows who he is or why he's there."

"He didn't have ID on him?" Cora said.

49

Harper snorted in disgust. "Typical. You won't tell me a damn thing, but you want to know what I know."

"Well, it would certainly help," Cora said. "I don't know how you expect me to discuss this crime without the facts."

"You expect to discuss the crime?"

"Absolutely, Chief. I would say in the next twenty-four hours everyone in Bakerhaven is going to be discussing the crime."

"That's not what I mean and you know it. How do you expect to discuss the crime if you won't tell me what you know?"

"Cora, do you know anything?" Becky said.

"No."

"In that case you wouldn't withhold it," Harper said.

"I'm not withholding it."

"You won't tell me why you were there."

"Yes. Suppose I stopped in to use the ladies' room. That would have nothing to do with the crime, but I wouldn't particularly want to discuss it."

"That's an abandoned filling station. The ladies' room is locked."

"How do you know? Did you check it?"

"Are you saying you used the ladies' room?"

"I just got through saying I didn't want to

discuss using the ladies' room."

"God save me. Becky, help me out here. I've got a dead body. I don't know who killed him. I don't even know who he is. Anything that would shed light on the situation would be helpful."

"Did you let Cora see the body?"

"She's already seen the body."

"I don't think that's a safe assumption, Chief. Since Cora isn't talking, there are any number of possibilities. It's possible she's seen the body and doesn't know who it is. It's possible she *hasn't* seen the body and doesn't know who it is. It's possible she *does* know who it is, but she hasn't seen the body yet, so she doesn't *know* she knows who he is."

"You left out the possibility she's seen the body and *already* knows who he is."

"Good point, Chief. If that were the case, and she isn't talking, nothing would help. But in case it isn't, I strongly suggest your showing her the body at the earliest convenience. Show her the body. In my presence, and without any attempt to trick her or trap her into an admission, and I'll allow her to make a statement."

"If I show her the body she'll talk?"

"She'll make a statement. She'll answer relevant questions."

"Who's going to decide what's relevant?"

"I am."

"What if I don't agree?"

"Well, then we can go hunt up Judge Hobbs, and he can explain to you how I'm her attorney and you're not. But why assume the worst? I'm assuming we look at the body, we have a nice discussion, and we go our separate ways. Isn't that how you see it, Cora?"

"For my money, you're being entirely too nice. He threw me in jail."

"I'm sure he's sorry. And I'm sure he realizes the concessions we're making in not adopting a hostile viewpoint."

Becky smiled at Chief Harper, who looked ready to snap her head off. He whipped out his cell phone. "Hey, Barney. Where's the stiff?"

CHAPTER 9

The Bakerhaven morgue was in a basement wing of the new hospital. Barney Nathan used to do autopsies in the back room of his private office, but the idea that there was a corpse just behind the door tended to make patients in the examining room a little nervous. There was the time the door blew open when Mrs. Sangstrum was changing. The naked woman was disconcerted to see a man in the next room, and not at all mollified when he turned out to be dead. Since then the doctor had conducted postmortems at the hospital.

Chief Harper had called ahead, so Barney Nathan was waiting for them. He bristled at the sight of Cora. "Is this necessary?" he said.

"They're not checking up on you, Barney," Chief Harper said. "Just trying to make an ID."

"You don't have one yet?"

"No. You got a cause of death?"

"You want me to spill it in front of them?"

"We're all friends here, Barney. And you know it's gonna be on the news."

"He was shot with a .38-caliber gun."

"You know the time of death?"

Barney made a face. "I'm not going to tell you that in front of the lawyer. For all I know, she might get me on the stand."

"I don't think there's much chance of that. Becky's representing Cora. Between you and me, I don't think she did it."

"Very funny, Chief," Cora said. "So, where's the bloody dead man?"

Harper frowned. "Bloody?"

"It's a quote, Chief. Don't be so damn literal."

"A quote?"

"From Dylan. So where is he?"

Barney Nathan led them over to a slab. The body on it was covered with a sheet.

"You finished?" Harper said.

Barney shook his head. "When I heard you coming, I covered him up."

"Okay, let's have a look."

Dr. Nathan pulled the sheet off the corpse's face.

Cora stepped up and took a look.

Becky Baldwin was right behind her.

"Interesting," Cora said.

Harper frowned. "Is that all you have to say?"

"It is in front of witnesses. You wanna tell the doctor to scram, we could talk."

Barney Nathan bristled with indignation. "This is my autopsy room. No one orders me out of my morgue."

"Of course not, Barney," Chief Harper said. "She's only trying to get your goat. Come on, Cora, let's go."

"I don't like to be ordered out of his morgue, either," Cora said.

Becky shot her a pleading look. They were in enough trouble already.

Harper ushered them upstairs and out the emergency room entrance. Evidently there were no emergencies at the moment. Both ambulances were standing by.

Harper stopped between parked cars.

"This is most informal," Cora said. "Does a statement made in a parking lot count?"

"All right," Harper said. "You've had a good look. Do you know who he is?"

"No, I don't."

"Have you ever seen him before?"

Cora shot a look at Becky. "Having seen him dead, I can now state unequivocally that I have never seen him alive."

Harper frowned. "What the hell does that mean?"

55

"It means I'm taking the question seriously and giving it every benefit of the doubt. Before I saw him, it was entirely possible I might have run into him someplace and just not known who he was. But that is not the case. I have not seen him in any social setting whatsoever. He is not someone I ever observed but was not introduced to. Or passed in the street either in Bakerhaven or elsewhere. In short, I do not know who this man is, and cannot help you in identifying him. Is that a fair statement of the facts, Becky?"

"Couldn't have said it better myself."

"Yes, you could," Harper said irritably. "You could have simply said I never saw the man before in my life. That would be a simple statement of the facts, without all the mumbo jumbo."

"But it might not be true," Cora said.

Harper scowled. "I beg your pardon?"

"I don't recognize him as anyone I ever met. But it's possible I've seen him and simply don't remember. For instance, if you were to produce witnesses that we had been at the same cocktail party, I would be hard pressed to deny it. Though I don't go to cocktail parties all that often since I quit drinking."

"You're not helping me," Harper cried in

exasperation. "You're talking a lot without saying anything. I want a straight answer. If you don't know the dead man, what were you doing at that service station?"

"Now there I would have to step in, Chief," Becky Baldwin said. "The question is based on a faulty premise. You're assuming that knowing the dead man and being at the service station are related. Since Cora doesn't know the dead man, obviously they're not. Therefore the question makes no sense."

"Fine," Harper said. "I'll simplify it. What were you doing at that service station?"

"There I would have to step in again. Since Cora doesn't know the dead man, her reason for being at the service station is totally irrelevant, and has no bearing on your investigation. So there is absolutely no reason for her to answer."

"I'll be the judge of that," Harper said. "Tell me why you were there, and *I'll* tell *you* if it has any bearing on the murder investigation."

"Sorry, Chief. We may be off the record, but we still have to play by the rules. I gather Cora doesn't wish to discuss her presence at the service station. On the other hand, she's perfectly willing to discuss your murder case."

"Fine," Harper said. He opened the back door of the police car, popped open his briefcase, pulled out a plastic evidence envelope. "Here you are. There was a puzzle found on the dead body. I'd like you to take a look at it, and tell me if you've ever seen *it* before. Is that all right with you, counselor? I'm not asking your client what *she* did at the filling station. I'm asking about a key piece of evidence in a murder case."

"There's a lot of puzzles in the world, Chief. How could she know if she'd seen this particular one?"

"She could if she recognized something about it. Then she could say yes. If she never saw anything like it, she could say no. If she happened to see the puzzle at the murder scene and wasn't sure if this was it, she could say I don't know. Doesn't that cover it?"

Becky smiled. "You're talking to a lawyer, Chief. I could give you half a dozen scenarios it doesn't cover."

"Great. Then you can tell me which case this happens to be. Well, Cora, have you ever seen this puzzle before?"

Cora steeled herself, hoped that she could make a truthful answer. In point of fact, she remembered the sudoku pretty well. She was pretty sure she'd recognize it.

Cora took the evidence envelope, looked at it.

Stared.

It was not the sudoku she had seen on the body of the dead man.

It was a crossword puzzle.

Across

1 Niagara Falls phenomenon
5 Saint with an alphabet named after him
10 1796 Napoleon victory site
14 Rights org. at the Scopes Trial
15 Spyri's Alpine orphan
16 Pundit's piece
17 Start of the hint

19 Be a rat
20 Musically monotonous
21 McGwire's 1998 homer count
23 Heredity unit
25 Where lts. are trained
26 Sheltering org.
30 Part 2 of the hint
35 To a higher degree
37 You're reading one
38 "Eureka!"
39 Year-end tune
40 Area of authority
42 Cow-horned goddess
43 Not Rx
44 Talk like a gangster
45 "Amscray!"
47 Part 3 of the hint
50 In great shape
51 Dapper guy?
52 Polishes off
54 Like some candles
58 Teased
63 Fontanne's partner
64 End of the hint
66 Bowed, on a score
67 Vacant, in a way
68 "Yeah, sure!"
69 Stadium vendor's load
70 Load of bull
71 Holy Week concludes it

Down

1 "Held" spread
2 Revered object
3 Veer
4 Veer
5 Place for laundry
6 From Mocha, e.g.
7 Umbrella part
8 Fateful time in the Forum
9 Trevi toss-ins, once
10 Far from cutting-edge
11 Time to hunt
12 Shoulder muscle, briefly
13 In a laid-back way
18 Shortage sign of the '70s
22 Stand up and be counted
24 Search dogs' quarry
26 Playground retort
27 Truth, to bards
28 Priority in rank
29 Disney collectible
31 Off one's feed
32 Ready for surgery, perhaps
33 Cologne's river
34 Slacked off
36 "The Plague" setting
41 Body shop fig.
42 "My turn!"
44 Payment from Ricky to Fred

46 And the following: Abbr.
48 Singer at shul
49 Blustery sort
53 Easily nettled
54 Marble hunk
55 Smoke or salt, e.g.
56 Big birds raised on farms
57 Word of warning
59 More than singular
60 Cut with a surgical beam
61 Title role for Julia
62 Nimble-fingered
65 __-Blo fuse

CHAPTER 10

Cora couldn't believe it. She exhaled slowly, buying time to think. The benign sudoku she could solve had turned into a poisonous crossword that she couldn't. Which was actually a relief. Now she didn't have to lie about having seen it before. She had never seen this puzzle before, and how it got on the dead man she couldn't begin to imagine. She could speak absolutely truthfully to Chief Harper on that score. So, in a way, the crossword was a blessing.

Except she couldn't solve the damn thing. How was she going to tap-dance her way out of that? Becky Baldwin knew she couldn't solve crosswords, although she still believed Cora constructed them. But Chief Harper didn't have a clue. As far as he knew, she was the Puzzle Lady, a celebrated cruciverbalist, whose puzzle-solving skills had often aided him in the past. He would expect them to do so again.

What the hell could she do?

"You say this was found on the body?"

"That's right."

"Who found it?"

Harper frowned. "Hey. I'm asking the questions here. And you're answering them. The more you evade, the more I think you have something to hide."

"Ask away. I'm not evading anything."

"Here's a puzzle. It was found on the body. I wanna know, without any evasions or double-talk, did you ever see it before?"

Cora put up her hand. "Let me get this one, Becky. In the spirit of cooperation, I would like to answer that question as simply and directly as possible. The answer is no. I have never seen it before in my life. Is that clear enough for you?"

"Yes, it is."

"Good. Can I go now? My niece is in this hospital having a baby, and I wanna be there."

"Sherry's having a baby right now?"

"Yes."

"What were you doing at an abandoned service station if your niece is having a baby?"

"There again, Chief," Becky said, "you are taking two unrelated statements and making them codependent. I wouldn't know how to answer such a question, and I'm certain my client doesn't."

"I don't," Cora said. "Can I go now?"

"You can go soon enough. At the moment, we're still talking about the puzzle."

"Well, I hope you don't expect her to solve it," Becky said. "That would be a little much. Arrest her and then ask her to do you a favor."

"I don't need her to solve it."

"Oh?"

"I figured that might be your attitude, so I had Dan Finley run a copy over to Harvey Beerbaum." Harper whipped out his cell phone, pushed speed-dial. "Dan. You get Harvey? Is he doing it? . . . Really? Great. I'm in the parking lot with Cora and Becky . . . No, we did not ID the body . . . No, we do not know who he is. You ask so many questions you'd think I worked for you." He snapped the phone shut. "Harvey solved the puzzle. Dan's on his way over with it."

"Then you don't need us," Cora said.

"Don't you wanna see the puzzle?"

"Not especially."

"A puzzle found with a dead body? Don't you care?"

"We get one of those every other week," Cora said.

"Well, you can take a look at this one. Here's Dan now."

Dan Finley drove into the lot, spotted the chief. He pulled up, hopped out of the car. "Got it, Chief. Not that it's gonna help."

"Why not?"

"It's just a stupid rhyme. Unless Cora knows what it means."

"Cora's not being cooperative," Harper said.

"Hey," Cora said. "You make me sound like a sulky ingrate. I happen to have been arrested."

"I'm sure the chief didn't mean it," Dan said. "You didn't mean it, did you, Chief?"

Harper looked ready to explode.

Becky stepped in suavely. "Since the puzzle's here, I think we can take a look at it. We're not obligating ourselves to anything. Cora's already stated that she's never seen it before. But we're perfectly happy to take a look at Harvey Beerbaum's solution. Isn't that right, Cora?"

"Happy is not the word."

"Let's not quibble. We're willing to take a look, so hand it over."

"Here it is." Dan handed the puzzle to Cora. "It's got me stumped. What do you think it means?"

"I think it means someone owes me an

apology," Cora said. "So, what's the theme entry?" she added, referring to the long answers the puzzle was built around. When confronted with crosswords, Cora always tried to use as many puzzle terms as possible, in order to create the illusion that she knew what she was talking about.

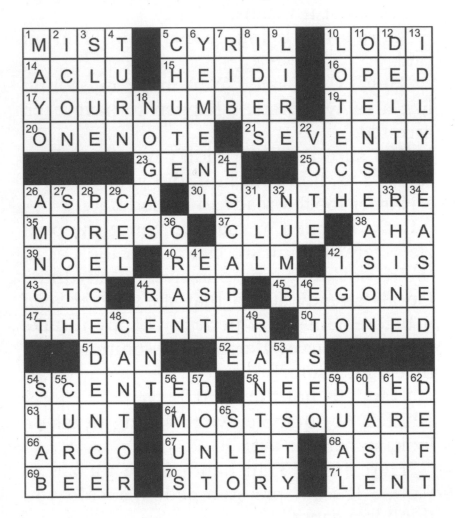

Cora scanned the puzzle. Read the theme entry aloud. "Your number is in there. The centermost square."

"What do you think it means?" Harper said.

"How the hell should I know?"

"Cora," Becky warned. She turned to the chief. "I have to agree with Dan. It's not very helpful." She pointed to the puzzle. "I mean, look. The center square doesn't *have* a number."

"It must be referring to something else," Harper said. "Do you have any idea what that might be?"

"Not really."

"Cora?"

"Not a clue."

"In the past you've found connections between crossword puzzles and sudokus."

"It's sudoku."

"Huh?"

"The plural of sudoku is sudoku. If that's confusing, you can call them sudoku puzzles."

"I don't care what you *call* them. I just care what they *do.*"

"They don't *do* anything, Chief. They're number puzzles."

"Cora," Becky said. "Not so hostile. I

think maybe the chief has something to tell us."

"Well, I don't," Harper said.

"You're not about to thrust a sudoku on us and demand to know how it fits in with the crossword?"

"No."

"Why not?"

"Because there doesn't happen to be one." Harper narrowed his eyes. "You wouldn't happen to know where one was, would you, Cora?"

Cora drew herself up. "I most certainly wouldn't. And I resent the implication."

"What implication?"

"I don't know. Whatever implication you were implying." Cora shook her head. "It's been a long day. You wanna give me a copy of this, and any other puzzles you might happen to find, I'm willing to check on them. But for the time being, I looked at the body, I made a full and frank statement. So, unless you wanna arrest me again, I'm gonna go see my niece."

CHAPTER 11

Cora found Aaron hanging out in the upstairs corridor. "Am I too late? I'll never forgive myself if I'm too late, but you wouldn't believe what happened. I can't tell you most of it, but some I can, and you'll probably want to print it." She broke off at the look on his face. "What's the matter?"

"There are complications."

"Complications? You mean the baby isn't born yet?"

"No."

"Then what are you doing here?"

"The doctors threw me out."

"Why?"

"It a breech."

"What?"

"It's a breech birth. The baby's turned the wrong way."

"So, what are they doing?"

"The doctors are trying to turn the baby. If they can, she can still deliver normally.

Otherwise, she'll have a C-section."

"That's not dangerous these days."

"No, but it stresses the baby. And it's premature anyway. A lot of things can go wrong."

Cora took him by the shoulders. "Yeah. But they're not going to. She's in the hospital. Under a doctor's care. Things are going to go right."

"Oh, yeah?" Aaron held up his iPhone. "You know how many things can go wrong in a breech birth? The umbilical cord gets wrapped around the baby. An arm or leg gets broken trying to turn it."

Cora snatched the iPhone from his hand. "That's the problem with the information age. Too much information." She thrust the phone deep into her floppy, drawstring purse.

"Hey, I need that."

"No, you don't. You can have it back when your baby's born. I gotta keep you off the Internet before you drive yourself nuts. Where's Sherry?"

"In the OR."

"OR? Good God, I don't know what happened to language these days. It's your damn phone. Everything sounds like a text message. I assume the OR is where they operate."

"That's right."

"Where is that?"

"Through there."

"Fine." Cora made for the door.

"You can't go in there."

"Oh, yeah? Who's gonna stop me?"

Actually, it was two orderlies and a scrub nurse. They deposited Cora unceremoniously in the corridor, stationed a security guard in the doorway to discourage any other visitors, and went back to rescrub.

"Told you," Aaron said.

Cora commented on the hospital's lack of hospitality.

"Did you see Sherry? Did you see anything?"

"Not a damn thing. Except a bunch of ruffled feathers. You'd think I'd breached the War Room." She made a face. "Didn't mean to say *breach*. Insensitive."

A doctor squeezed past the security guard out into the corridor. A surgical mask hung from his neck. He flinched slightly at the sight of Cora, and walked up to Aaron Grant.

"How is she?"

"She's fine. The baby's fine. We're going to do a Caesarian section. Anything else is too risky for the baby. But this is just routine. We can do a bikini cut, she'll still look good in a bathing suit."

"You think I care about that now!" Aaron cried. He controlled himself. Still breathing heavily, he said, "If you're operating on her, what are you doing out here?"

The doctor smiled. "I came to get you. At this point, it's a routine surgery. You can be there for the delivery."

Cora opened her mouth.

"Just the husband," he added quickly.

CHAPTER 12

Cora found Becky waiting in the lobby.

"What's happening?" Becky said.

"Sherry's having a C-section. The baby's a breech. Aaron's in there with her."

"Why did you have me wait?"

"We have a problem."

"No kidding. I need to get back to the office."

"Not yet."

"Why not?"

"Come outside."

Becky followed Cora out front. "All right, what is it?"

Cora grimaced. "Well, I didn't tell you everything."

"What?"

"It's a complicated case. So many little details."

"What little detail are you referring to?" Becky said.

Cora told Becky about finding the sudoku

on the dead man's body.

"That's a *little* detail?" Becky said incredulously.

"Let's not quibble over size. The point is, I found a sudoku on the body. Miraculously, it changed into a crossword puzzle."

"That's why you were asking Chief Harper about a sudoku."

"I was afraid he was going to spring it on me. Ask if I'd ever seen it before."

"At which point, *as your lawyer,* I would have been able to advise you how to answer the question," Becky said dryly. "If I'd known about it. As things stood, I wouldn't have had a clue."

"It's a moot point. He didn't ask."

"Yeah. Why do you suppose he didn't?"

"Only one thing I can figure."

"What's that?"

"He didn't find it."

"How is that possible?"

"I have a theory."

"I'm sure you do. Care to share it?"

"When I found the sudoku I was in a bit of a spot. I was tempted to take it. But I already had the blackmail money on me. It didn't seem like a good time to be caught removing evidence from a crime scene."

"Just what *is* a good time to be caught removing evidence from a crime scene?"

Becky said dryly.

"So I stuck it back in his pocket for Chief Harper to find. Only when he does it's a crossword puzzle. Which is nice, because I could honestly say I never saw it."

"Forget all that. Where's the sudoku?"

"Well, either Chief Harper found it and isn't letting on, or it's still in the coat."

"Which the cops searched."

"Right."

"How can that be?"

"I've got no idea. But it's gotta be one or the other."

"Anyone else at the crime scene who could have taken it?"

"Just Dr. Smarty-Pants."

"Why would he do that?"

"He wouldn't."

"So it's gotta be the cops."

"Unless it isn't."

Becky looked at Cora in exasperation. "What's your point?"

Cora jerked her thumb at the hospital. "Barney Nathan."

"What about him?"

"You think he's gay?"

Becky stared at her. "What?"

"Do you think Barney Nathan's gay?"

"He's got a wife and kids."

"Not always a deal breaker. But he's married?"

"You didn't know that?"

"I only keep track of the marital status of potential suitors."

"And Barney isn't?"

"I have a habit of pointing out flaws in his autopsies. After three times, men don't usually ask you out. So, Barney's heterosexual."

"Yeah. So?"

"And you're the impossible dream. Every man's secret fantasy. The stunning super-model, too pretty to approach."

"What the hell are you talking about?"

Cora made a face. "Come on. Just because you look like a beautiful airhead doesn't mean you have to think like one. You're a lawyer. Think like a lawyer."

"Why? What do you want?"

"I want you to seduce Barney Nathan."

CHAPTER 13

Dr. Barney Nathan was washing his hands in the morgue sink.

Becky Baldwin stuck her head in the door. "Excuse me?"

The doctor looked up. Frowned. "What is it?"

Becky pushed her way into the room. "Sorry to bother you. I just have a couple of questions."

Barney shook his head. "That's not appropriate. You're a lawyer. I'm the medical examiner."

Becky leaned in, gave him her hundred-watt smile. "This is strictly off the record. Just between you and me."

The top button of her blouse popped open. This was not unexpected. Cora had unbuttoned the button halfway so the slightest pressure would finish the job. While hardly revealing, the effect was wildly suggestive.

Barney blinked. "Off the record?"

"Absolutely." Becky put her hand on his arm. "I wouldn't want you to get the wrong idea. Cora's my client, but she's . . . well, Cora. You know what I mean?"

"I certainly do."

"But I would prefer if that didn't put a strain between us. It's a small town. We all have to live here."

"Of course."

"I'd like to come to an understanding. Could I buy you a cup of coffee?"

"I have to finish the autopsy."

"You look like you're done."

"I still have to write it up. Bag his things for the police."

"Don't the police already have the evidence?"

"They have the evidence. They want his clothes. I don't know why. I suppose you could get DNA from them." Barney made a face. "See, that's why I shouldn't be talking to you. That's the type of thing you'd pick on in a trial. Why the cops didn't have it sooner."

Becky smiled. "And I'd have to testify it was my fault because the reason was I was buying you a cup of coffee. Come on, Barney. Cora Felton's giving you a hard

80

time? I could tell you a few things about her."

Barney Nathan was smiling as they went out.

Cora waited until the elevator door closed on them, then slipped out of the medical supply closet and made her way down the corridor.

The door to the morgue was locked.

Damn. She should have had Becky wedge something in it on her way out to keep it open. Not that Becky wouldn't have balked at the idea. It had been hard enough persuading her to buy the doctor a cup of coffee.

She had to pry the lock. Impossible to do without leaving a trace, but there was no help for it. The cops would know someone had broken in, they just wouldn't know why.

With luck, they wouldn't know who.

Cora looked around for something to jimmy the door. Nothing sprang to mind. The corridor seemed remarkably devoid of burglary equipment.

Her eyes lit on the door of the medical supply closet. There must be something in there. A scalpel, a forceps, a set of lock picks, or something.

Cora hurried to the supply room door, flung it open.

A janitor came around the corner. He stopped and frowned. Cora Felton didn't look like a doctor or a nurse. She looked like a snoopy old lady poking around in the medical supplies.

Cora smiled ruefully, shook her head. "This isn't the morgue. I left my keys in the morgue. Dr. Nathan said I could run down and get them. But this isn't it. Do you know where the morgue is?"

The janitor pointed. "End of the corridor."

"Oh," Cora said. "I got confused."

"I see," the janitor said. Clearly he didn't. The doors didn't look at all alike.

Cora hurried to the door, tried the knob. She turned back to the janitor. "It's locked."

"Then the doctor's not there."

"I know he's not there. I just left him upstairs in the cafeteria. He told me to go get them. He must have forgotten he locked it."

"He always locks it."

Cora grimaced. "Just because he's a doctor doesn't mean he's bright." She pretended to notice for the first time the keys dangling from the janitor's belt. "You've got keys for everything, don't you? You can let me in."

"I'm not supposed to let people in."

"You're not supposed to let people in *without permission.* The doctor *told* me to go in."

The janitor scratched his head. "I don't know."

"You wanna ask him? He's sitting in the cafeteria with a knockout of a young blonde. Which is probably why he forgot the door was locked, and was so eager to get me away from the table. You wanna ask him, fine, but I don't think he's gonna be glad to see you."

The janitor wavered. Cora thought she had him. Then he shook his head. "No, you better get the keys from him."

Cora made a face. "Then I'll have to bother him twice. To give them back. How about he okays it, and you let me in? Come on. Only take you a minute."

The janitor was severely overmatched. Cora was already dragging the poor man to the elevator. Before he knew what was happening she had thrust him in and pushed the button.

As the door opened on the first floor she realized she had no idea where the cafeteria was. "Which way is the lunchroom? I always get turned around in elevators."

"This way."

She batted her eyes at the janitor. Realized he wasn't as old as she'd first thought.

"Thank you. I'm so bad with directions. And I hate to waste your time. Right down here?"

"To the left."

Cora spotted the door to the cafeteria. "Ah. Here we are. I hope he's not too mad at me."

Cora pushed open the door, looked around. She was in luck. Becky and the doctor were seated out of earshot at the far end of the room. Becky was talking animatedly. Dr. Nathan was hanging on her every word.

"He's not going to be happy," Cora said. "I'll try not to let on you're the one who's asking." She raised her voice. "Oh, Dr. Nathan!"

Barney Nathan looked up. He clearly was not pleased.

Cora smiled and waved.

The doctor made a dismissive gesture, and turned back to Becky Baldwin.

"Oh, dear," Cora said. "He wants me to handle it myself. I'm afraid you'll have to talk to him."

The janitor frowned. Barney Nathan had resumed his conversation. The thought of disturbing the doctor did not thrill him. "Okay. I'll let you in. But just to get your keys. I got work to do."

"Of course, of course."

Cora was pleased with herself. Barney Nathan thought she was just being nosy. He hadn't even noticed the janitor standing there, so he wouldn't ask him what she wanted. And the janitor would never bring it up to the doctor that he'd let someone in the lab. So far, so good.

Now she just had to get rid of him.

They went back downstairs. The janitor unlocked the door.

Cora pushed by him, strode up to the slab. "Now, let's see. I left them right here by the body, and —" She feigned surprise. "No. Wait a minute. Chief Harper was asking the doctor about the time element. He'd already covered him up with the sheet. You don't suppose it's under the sheet, do you?"

Cora pulled the cover off the dead man's face.

The janitor looked sick.

"No, not here."

She pulled the sheet farther down, revealed the eviscerated torso.

The janitor convulsed and turned away.

"Not here, either. Now what did I do with them?"

Cora's eyes widened. "Wait a minute. That's not the same body. Barney must have started another autopsy So where the hell's the corpse?"

Cora glanced around the room. Her eyes lit on the gleaming handles where metal trays with bodies pulled out from the wall. "There's the stiffs. I don't know which one's him. We'll have to check them all. Wanna help me? It'll go twice as fast. Come on. They don't smell as bad as you'd think."

The janitor was green around the gills. "You can handle it," he said, and beat a hasty retreat.

Cora went back to the victim on the slab. The clothes of course had been removed for the autopsy. She pulled the sheet all the way down, just in case they were folded up at the bottom of the slab. Was not surprised they weren't.

So where were they?

A metal hamper held only used lab coats. A metal drawer held only clean lab coats. A metal locker held a medical bag, presumably Dr. Nathan's. If so, the good doctor had neglected to lock it, no doubt figuring the lock on the morgue door would be enough.

A plastic container underneath the sink supplied the answer. It occurred to Cora the storing of evidence where it might get wet would be a handy thing to have on cross-examination.

Cora pulled out the bin, set it on an empty

examining table. Took off the plastic top. Damn. They'd have to concede the storage bin under the sink had a top. Maybe it was leaky.

It was disappointingly airtight. Cora wrenched it off, pored through the clothes. The jacket was on the bottom. She wondered if it would be important to get them back in the proper order. The doctor would be unlikely to notice, still, he might have a standard routine. The jacket on the bottom figured. It would come off first.

Cora was not daydreaming while she was thinking all this. She had already jerked the jacket out and was digging through the pockets. She was pretty sure the puzzle was in the left inside breast pocket, but there was nothing there. Or in the right inside breast pocket. Not that there should have been — the police had searched the coat.

She turned it inside out, looked at the lining. It was an off-green color, not to Cora's taste, but aside from that it looked fine.

She squeezed it.

It crinkled.

Cora pulled at the fabric. There was a slit in the lining just above the pocket. It only showed if you stretched the lining down. She thrust her hand in, grabbed the piece

of paper, pulled it out.
   It was the sudoku.

CHAPTER 14

There was no one in the corridor upstairs. Cora didn't crash the OR again, just hunted up the nurses' station and asked for Sherry's room number. Apparently it wasn't visiting hours, and the nurse on duty was reluctant to give it. Luckily, she knew Cora as the Puzzle Lady, and granted her celebrity status.

Cora wasn't sure if having Sherry's room number implied that Sherry was in it, but it didn't seem prudent to press the point. She left the nurses' station, set off to find out on her own.

Cora knocked gently, stuck her head in the door.

Sherry was lying in bed asleep. Aaron was sitting next to her holding her hand.

Cora's heart fluttered.

There was no baby in sight.

"Aaron," Cora whispered. "What happened?"

Aaron put his finger to his lips. "She did great. She's fine. The baby's fine."

"Where's the baby?"

"ICU. Being checked out. They say it's routine after a traumatic birth."

"Traumatic?"

"Well, it wasn't any picnic. They tried like hell to avoid a Caesarian."

"The baby's okay?"

"The baby's fine."

"Can I see her?"

"They won't let you."

"Then I gotta go. Becky's got this case."

"Go on. I'll tell her you were here."

"You need anything?"

"I'm fine."

"They're not going to bring the baby in?"

"Not for a while."

"In that case, you can have your cell phone." Cora fished it out of her drawstring purse, tossed it to the young reporter. "Soon as we can see the baby, call Becky and I'll come back."

"What's the case?"

"Nothing you can write. But I gotta go see her."

Cora went out and hunted up the intensive care unit. Security was not as good as at the OR. Cora was halfway across the room before anyone confronted her.

A soft woman in scrubs almost apologetically informed her she couldn't be there.

"I'm looking for the Grants' baby," Cora said. "I don't know whether it's under Sherry Grant, Sherry Carter, or Sherry Carter Grant, but, whatever it is, she had a baby, and they tell me it's here."

"You can't be here."

"Why not?"

"You're not sterile."

"I'm not going to touch anything. I just wanna see the kid. The kid's all right, isn't it? I mean, you're not stopping me from seeing the kid because something's wrong? That's not why it's having intensive care? There's nothing wrong?"

"I'd have to look at the chart."

"Look at the chart. Look at the chart."

The doctor went over to an incubator, took the clipboard off the hook.

Cora peered over her shoulder.

The baby looked small, wrinkly.

"Why is it in an incubator?" Cora demanded.

"Because the microwave was busy."

Cora's mouth fell open.

The doctor smiled. "The baby's fine. It's just being monitored."

"Why?"

"It's premature, for one thing. We have to

be sure the lungs are fully developed."

"Are they?"

"There's no indication that they're not. But we take nothing for granted here."

Cora was barely listening. She was looking at the baby.

"Oh, you poor little thing." She shook her head, smiled. Her eyes were misty. "You don't even know there's such a thing as men."

CHAPTER 15

Becky Baldwin was indignant. "You *left* me there," she accused.

"I didn't leave you there."

"Oh? What do *you* call it, then?"

"I said keep him busy. I didn't say forever."

"But you never came back."

"Why would I come back?"

"To tell me you were finished. To let me off the hook. I'd probably still be there if his wife hadn't called."

"Oh?"

"You should have seen him blush. His face was as red as his bow tie."

"You're a heartless home wrecker. Console yourself with the thought any time you start doubting your allure."

"Even then I didn't know if it was safe to let him go."

"You couldn't use your own judgment?"

"How would you like it if Barney Nathan

walked in on you rifling the morgue?"

"You think I was going to hang out with the corpses? I got in and got out."

"And how was I to know that? If you didn't find it, I was afraid you'd keep looking."

"I found it."

"Where was it?"

"What do you mean?"

Becky blinked. "That's a direct question. I don't think I could be more explicit."

"Yeah, but do you want to know the answer?" Cora reached in her purse. "It just so happens that I have a Xerox copy of a sudoku. I can tell you where *that* came from. It came from a copy machine on the second floor. I doubt if knowing that is going to get you into any trouble."

"Did you solve it?"

"Yeah."

"And?"

"Believe it or not, it happens to be a collection of eighty-one numbers ranging from one to nine."

"Which one is in the center square?"

"Here, take a look."

Cora handed her the sudoku.

9	5	1	2	6	8	7	3	4
4	6	8	7	3	1	5	9	2
3	7	2	4	9	5	1	6	8
1	2	4	3	5	9	8	7	6
6	9	7	1	8	4	2	5	3
5	8	3	6	2	7	4	1	9
7	1	9	8	4	6	3	2	5
8	3	6	5	1	2	9	4	7
2	4	5	9	7	3	6	8	1

"Eight?" Becky said. "What does that mean?"

"I have no idea."

"Maybe there's a clue in the puzzle."

"The clue in the puzzle says look in the center square."

"Maybe there's something else."

"Well, we can look for it later," Cora said. "At the moment, we don't have time."

"Why not?"

"It so happens I need your help."

"Doing what?"

Cora smiled and shrugged. "Compounding a felony and conspiring to conceal a crime."

CHAPTER 16

Becky drove slowly past the abandoned filling station. The crime scene ribbon was still up, but there was no one guarding it.

"Well, that's a fine state of affairs," Cora said. "Anyone could come along and rob that garbage bin."

"Or plant evidence," Becky said dryly.

"Good thinking. Is there anything you'd care to plant?"

"We're in enough trouble as it is."

"Exactly," Cora said. "We're in so deep another charge or two isn't going to matter."

"It matters to me. It matters to the bar association."

"A bunch of stuffy old lawyers? Who cares what they think?"

"You're not amusing me, Cora."

"Well, it's hard to be amusing when you don't know which end is up. If you'd care to let me in on the case."

"There is no case. There's a blackmail demand. We tried to deal with it. It didn't work."

"There's a hell of an understatement. You wanna turn around before we wind up in Danbury?"

They had driven quite a ways. Becky pulled into a driveway, turned the car, drove back again.

"No one's there," Cora said.

"That's what they want us to think," Becky told her.

"Who?"

"The police."

"Are you kidding me? Chief Harper, Dan Finley, and Sam Brogan? You think I couldn't spot one of them?"

"Well, when you put it that way."

"There's obviously no one there," Cora said. "I'm going in."

"How do you want to do this?"

"Quickly and without a hitch."

"No. I mean should I drive in?"

"Not unless you have a death wish. Drive on by, park in the street close to the Dumpster."

"Why?"

"Why do you think?"

Becky drove by the service station, pulled up to the curb. Cora slipped out of the passenger seat, hopped up onto the sidewalk.

Grass had grown up around the abandoned lot. Cora avoided it, stayed on the pavement, went up the driveway. She slipped under the crime scene ribbon, went straight to the Dumpster, raised the lid. She leaned over, reached to the bottom, made frantic searching motions. She straightened up, flopped the lid down, and plunged her hand into her drawstring purse. She turned, crouching low in the shadows, and hotfooted it back to the car.

Cora slipped into the passenger seat and said, "Let's get out of here!"

"What the hell did you just do?"

"Searched the Dumpster."

"What for?"

"A clue."

"The police already searched the Dumpster."

"Yeah. And if they're watching now, I wanna get arrested for searching the crime scene, not leading them to the money."

"You think they'd arrest us?"

"They will if you drive off. If they don't, they're not here, and we can get the money. Come on. Let's go."

Becky pulled out and drove down the road. No one arrested them. No one seemed to be paying the least bit of attention.

"All right," Cora said. "Let's go get the money."

Becky turned the car, drove back. "Where do you want me to park this time?"

"Pull up next to the gas pump."

"Why?"

"I'm going to crouch down behind the car so no one can see what I'm doing."

"I thought no one was looking."

"No one *is* looking. You wanna dance naked on the hood of the car? You can. No one's watching. But it's probably not a good idea."

"Fine. Just get the money, will you? You're making me nervous."

"You're nervous? How do you think I feel?"

"Come on. You play fast and loose with the law all the time."

"Sure. For other people. I'm always innocent. This time I happen to be guilty."

"Bite your tongue."

Becky pulled up next to the pumps.

Cora grimaced. "You couldn't have come in from the other side?"

"I thought this *was* the side."

"It's the right side of the *pump.* Wrong side of the *car.* When I step out the door it won't be shielding me. I gotta go all the way around."

"Oh. Huge imposition."

"It is if I get caught."

"So don't get caught."

"Why'd you pull in this way?"

"The gas tank's on this side."

"Are you kidding me? This is an abandoned station. It's not like we're buying gas." Still muttering, Cora got out of the car and stomped around to the pump.

She put her hands on the panel and pulled.

It gave, but not that much. Cora'd had no problem bending it before, motivated by fear. Where was that motivation now? Perhaps a police car driving by?

Even the thought of the authorities wasn't enough. The metal wasn't bending.

Was this the right pump?

That paranoid thought tipped the scale. The metal gave. Her hand reached in. Touched . . .

Nothing!

There was nothing there. The package had slipped down. And now the metal was pinning her arm.

"Becky!" Cora hissed.

Becky rolled the window down. "You got it?"

"No, I don't have it. I need help."

"You're kidding."

"Get out of the car."

Becky slipped out of the driver's seat. "What's the matter?"

"My arm's trapped. I need you to help pull the metal back so I can reach the money."

"Oh, for goodness' sake." Becky grabbed the plate, pulled.

Cora's arm was numb. It took a second to realize she was free. She reached deeper into the gas pump. Her hand hit a solid sheet of metal. The bottom of the panel.

"Damn."

"What?"

"It's not there."

"What?"

Cora pulled her arm out. "It's not there."

"Are you sure?"

"Absolutely."

"Maybe it was the other pump."

"No, it was this pump."

"Are you sure?"

"Yes, I'm sure."

Cora moved to the other pump, started prying at the panel.

"What are you doing?"

"Checking the other pump."

"I thought you were sure."

"I *am* sure. I'll be more sure after I check the pump."

"Then you're not sure."

"I'm sure. Help me bend the damn panel."

The panel on the second pump didn't bend as easily as the first, a good indication it hadn't been bent before. Cora searched it anyway. To absolutely no avail.

The money was gone.

CHAPTER 17

Becky was clearly shaken. She tossed off her scotch on the rocks, signaled for another.

Cora and Becky were sitting in a booth in the bar of the Country Kitchen, the popular home-style restaurant where Cora played bridge on Thursday nights. Upon not finding the money, Becky had driven straight there and was fortifying herself with scotch. She took a gulp, swallowed. "How could this have happened?"

"You know how it happened. The blackmailer was waiting for me to make the drop. He saw me hide the money in the pump, he waited till the cops left, and took it."

"You're assuming the blackmailer got the money?"

"Unless the blackmailer's the body in the Dumpster."

Becky said nothing.

"*Is* the blackmailer the body in the Dumpster?"

"I would think not."

"You would *think* not?"

"Well, I don't think *so*. If it were, who killed him?"

"If it *weren't*, who killed him? Come on, Becky. It's one thing holding out on me in a blackmail. Now you're holding out on me in a murder."

"I don't know anything about the murder. I don't know who this guy is. I don't know why he's dead."

"You know about the blackmail."

"We don't know if the blackmail and the murder are connected."

"You think it's a coincidence? The killer just chose the blackmail drop sight to dump his dead body?"

"I think there's *some* connection, but it doesn't have to be direct."

"Despite the fact the killer made off with the money."

"We don't know that."

"Oh? It was some *third* unconnected party who did that?" Cora rubbed her forehead. "It's times like this I wish I hadn't quit drinking. Then I watch you pouring it down."

"You want me to stop?"

"No, I want you to get good and drunk, and then you can tell me what you can't tell me sober."

"It's not that I don't want to tell you."

"Right. You can't betray the confidence of a client." Cora snorted. "Though I can't imagine how much confidence the client's going to have with the way you're handling this."

"That's a different kind of confidence. As a wordsmith, you should know that."

Cora took a breath. "Let's assume I'm not a wordsmith. I'm a private investigator. In your employ. In your service."

"That's a hot one. All you've managed to do is lose the money."

"Oh, now it's my fault? You think I should have kept it on me? With the police catching me at a murder scene?"

"Of course not," Becky said. "I'm not thinking straight. It's the worst predicament of my legal career. Cut me a little slack."

"I'll say you're not thinking straight. You don't know if the blackmail and the murder are connected. The blackmailer sent a sudoku. The killer sent a sudoku. Therefore the blackmailer is the killer."

"Unless the blackmailer *planted* the sudoku on the victim's body."

Cora rolled her eyes. "Oh, my God, you've drunk the Kool-Aid. The blackmailer, inconvenienced by the presence of a corpse in the very place he chose for the money drop, tries to incorporate it into his plan by planting puzzles on the body. Would you like to explain to me how that comes to pass?"

"I don't know how it comes to pass. I don't know how any of this comes to pass. Can't you see I'm very upset?"

Cora shrugged.

"Hadn't noticed."

CHAPTER 18

Sherry was propped up in bed. She managed a brief smile when Cora poked her head in the door.

"Well, that's more like it," Cora said. "The last time I came to see you you were no fun at all."

"I'm fine. Except they won't let me see my baby."

"Of course not. You're all doped up. You'd drop her on her head."

"She's in the ICU."

"I see you, too," Cora said. "It doesn't mean you're strong enough to hold the baby."

"Stop it," Sherry said.

"She's not in the mood," Aaron put in protectively.

"I'm upset. I want to see my baby."

"I've seen your baby. She's fine."

"She's not fine. She had a trauma."

"She's over it. She winked at me."

"Babies don't wink."

"This one did. We have a special bond. I'm the good aunt Cora, letting her do the things nasty Mama won't."

Sherry tried to smile, couldn't, turned her head.

Cora came up to the bed, took Sherry's hand and squeezed it. "Not buying the shtick, huh, kid? Well, buck up. It's a happy moment. You're a mommy."

Sherry choked back a sob. "I want to see my baby."

"I'll see what I can do."

Cora went back to the ICU. They were ready for her this time. A doctor, a nurse, and two interns met her at the door.

"No security guard?" Cora said. "I suppose you've got him on speed-dial."

The doctor was a stern-looking woman. "This is the ICU. You can't come in."

"Why not?"

"You're not sterile."

"I'll wash my hands and put on a mask."

"Sorry."

"But I'm her aunt."

The doctor shook her head. "Not close enough. Parent or sibling. Even then we'd talk you out of it."

"It's not like I'm going to take her out and play with her," Cora said. "I just want to look."

"Sorry."

Cora put her arm around the doctor's shoulders. "All right, look, doc. My niece is in hysterics because she can't see her kid. She thinks the baby's dying or something. She needs reassurance. Can't you roll it into her room just for a minute? Let her get a look."

"No way. The baby's premature, it's had a trauma, and it can't be moved. It's not dying or anything, but it's not being bumped down the hallway into someone's room. The baby's not up to that."

"Oh." Cora cocked her head, leaned in confidentially. "You got one that *is?*"

The doctor's mouth fell open.

Cora walked back into Sherry's room followed by two interns with a gurney.

"What's going on?" Aaron said.

"Absolutely nothing," Cora said.

The interns descended on Sherry. One slipped a surgical mask over her face. The other began unhooking the IV bags from the bed and attaching them to the pole on the gurney.

"You're going for a little ride, kid," Cora said, "but we're pretending you're not. At least, we're pretending you're not you. If there's a doctor in the hall, you keep your head down, I'll go into my these-are-not-the-droids-you're-looking-for routine."

"What?"

"You're a post-op patient who's not supposed to be moved. That's why we're not moving you."

The interns slid Sherry onto the gurney, covered her with a sheet.

Cora poked her head out in the corridor, signaled all-clear. The interns wheeled the gurney out and down the hall.

The doctor was waiting at the door to the ICU. She grabbed the clipboard off the gurney. "Is this the patient?"

"Yes."

"Ah, yes. Another post-op. Wheel her in. We'll find room."

The interns wheeled Sherry in. Cora and Aaron tried to follow, but the doctor shook her head and closed the door.

"Well, now," the doctor said, "you seem a little old for pediatric ICU, but who am I to judge? Bring her over here, will you?"

The interns wheeled the gurney over to the incubator.

Sherry raised her head to look.

The doctor pushed her back. "Easy. I'm taking enough chances here without you pulling any stitches. Let them help you."

The interns raised the end of the gurney.

111

Sherry looked over at the incubator. Inside was a tiny baby. Her baby. It was flailing its arms and legs, to which monitor sensors were attached.

Sherry wasn't paying any attention. Her eyes were fixed on the beautiful little baby behind the Plexiglas.

"Jennifer," she murmured.

"Hmm?"

"Her name is Jennifer."

"Nice name."

Sherry sucked in her breath. "Oh!"

"What is it?"

"She winked at me."

CHAPTER 19

Early the next morning Cora Felton was on her way into the hospital when Becky Baldwin came roaring up and intercepted her in the parking lot. Becky clearly had not slept well. Her hair was disheveled and her eyes were bloodshot. She still looked good, just not in an airbrushed-photo way.

"Hop in," Becky said.

"I'm going to see Sherry."

"Later. We got trouble."

"What do you mean, we?"

"Just get in."

Cora walked around the car and got in. Becky took off.

"Hey!" Cora said. "Where are you going?"

"Nowhere. I just can't sit still. I'm going to drive around while you look at this."

"Look at what?"

Becky passed her a folded sheet of paper.

Cora unfolded it. Her eyes widened. She read, " 'I looked in the Dumpster. The

113

money wasn't there. I'm getting angry. I want my ten grand, and I want it now. So. Last chance. New time. Nine P.M. New place. Solve the puzzles to find out where.' "

"Puzzles? What puzzles?"

Becky passed them over.

A crossword and a sudoku.

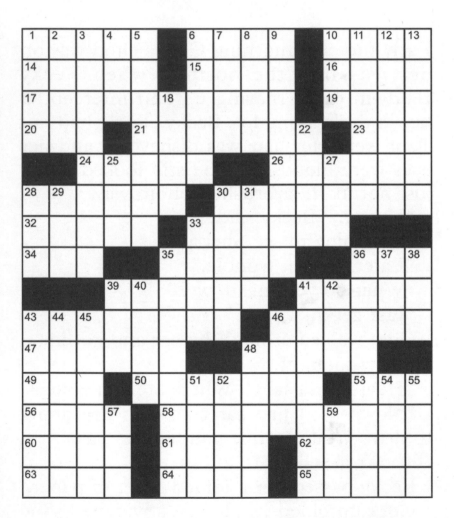

Across

1 Headstone's place
6 Chilled out
10 Some Feds
14 Absorb a loss, slangily
15 Big Apple stage award
16 Harry Chapin hit
17 Start of the hint
19 "Chocolat" costar
20 T size: Abbr.
21 What ungentlemanly sorts have
23 Soccer stadium cheer
24 "Fighting" team
26 Stivic player
28 "Soon . . ."
30 Part 2 of the hint
32 Bugs of the underworld
33 Nose-in-the-air sorts
34 MLB bigwigs
35 Go off the rail
36 In honor of
39 Haunted house sound
41 Hymn of praise
43 Part 3 of the hint
46 Some cameras
47 Made amends
48 After-class aide
49 Do-over at Ashe
50 Vacationers' hirees

53 Incarcerated Nobel Peace Prize winner
56 Area between gutters
58 End of the hint
60 "The Heat __" (Frey tune)
61 Screws up
62 Seating selection
63 Witches' brew ingredient
64 Place for a buggy
65 Exodus figure

Down

1 Figures out
2 Barack's first Chief of Staff
3 Places for canvases
4 London's Old __
5 Prince William, e.g.
6 Scungilli source
7 Third man in Genesis
8 Maltese monetary unit, once
9 Where sailors dine
10 Muscle car of old
11 "Cheers" proprietor
12 Sends to Siberia
13 West Coast gridders, informally
18 Like some outlooks
22 On its way
25 Vitamin label letters
27 Uncertainties
28 Chat room "Yikes!"

29 __ de guerre
30 How losses appear
31 Man the chuck wagon
33 Spanker, e.g.
35 Unlike movie extras
36 Unflinching
37 Cask material
38 ICU staffers
39 Roget's entry: Abbr.
40 Hotfoots it
41 1945 conference site
42 Commotion
43 Like many talk radio shows
44 Relaxing
45 "Maybe tomorrow"
46 Northern Iraqi
48 Play pranks on
51 Word after see- or drive-
52 Gull kin
54 Maroon's home
55 Plays for a sap
57 Sinus specialist, briefly
59 Popular cruise stop

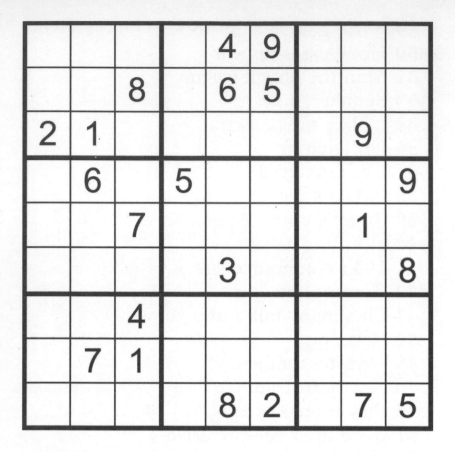

"Ah, hell!" Cora said.

"Yeah," Becky said. "And I know you can't solve the crossword."

"And Sherry's in the hospital."

"Is she coherent? Could she do it?"

"Sure, but if I tried to take it to her, Aaron would swoop down like an avenging fury and rip my head off."

"So who are we going to take it to?"

"I'm afraid there's only one choice."

"You mean . . . ?"

"Yeah," Cora said grimly. "Harvey Beer-baum."

CHAPTER 20

While Cora was a fake cruciverbalist, Harvey Beerbaum was the genuine article. He constructed crosswords, he competed in tournaments, he contributed to the *New York Times.*

He also was infatuated with Cora Felton, which drove her to distraction. There were few men Cora would not deign to marry, but Harvey topped the list. Bald, portly, fastidious, precise, he projected as so effeminate Cora sometimes wondered if his pursuit of her was just for show.

Harvey had come to her aid in the past. He knew she couldn't solve puzzles. He didn't know she couldn't construct them, either.

Harvey lived in a gingerbread house, quaintly furnished with crossword puzzle memorabilia, including a trophy for coming in seventh in the Nationals, and framed copies of autographed puzzles by such noted constructors as Maura Jacobson and Merl Reagle.

Only two things were bothering him.

Cora had brought along a lawyer.

And he'd already been asked to solve one puzzle by the police.

"Let me get you some tea," Harvey said, inviting them to sit down.

"Don't go to any trouble," Becky said.

"Oh, it's no trouble. Let me put on the kettle. You can choose your own tea. Lemon Zinger. Sleepytime. Earl Grey."

Harvey thrust a basket of tea bags on the table. Slid saucers and spoons in front of them.

"There now. We have a minute while this boils. Tell me what this is all about. You say you have a puzzle."

"Yes," Cora said.

"Which you would like me to solve?" He posed the question delicately.

"It's all right," Cora said. "Becky knows I can't solve crosswords. She's my lawyer. I can't hold out on her. It's lawyer/client privilege, and she won't tell. Just as we have cruciverbalist privilege."

His eyes twinkled. "Well put. You have a puzzle?"

"Yes."

"The police have also brought me a

121

puzzle."

"So I hear."

"Connected to the murder."

"That's Chief Harper's theory."

"You don't think so?"

"I don't know the facts."

"That's strange."

"Why?"

"Chief Harper brought the puzzle to me. Normally he would have brought it to you. So there must be a reason. The only one I can think of is you must be involved."

"I'm not involved."

"According to Chief Harper you were at the crime scene."

Cora smiled. "That doesn't mean I'm involved. It just means I'm nosy. Come on, Harvey. You know me. You think I'm involved in a murder?"

"Of course not."

"Well, there you are."

The teakettle whistled.

Harvey brought it to the table, filled the cups. "Milk? Sugar? Lemon?" he offered.

"Yeah, all of that," Cora said.

Harvey looked horrified. "You can't mix milk with lemon. It curdles."

"Oh. Is that why my tea always looks funny?"

Harvey cut a lemon, brought the sugar

bowl and a pitcher of milk to the table.

Becky took lemon.

Cora took milk and sugar.

"There, Harvey," Cora said. "Nothing curdled. Can we talk to you about this puzzle?"

"I'd like to talk to you about the other puzzle. I assume you've seen it."

"Why do you assume that?"

"Well, I couldn't make any sense out of it, so I assume Chief Harper showed it to you."

"He did."

"And?"

"And it didn't make any sense to me, either."

"It seemed to be referring to a sudoku. Is that how it seemed to you?"

"It's possible."

"Chief Harper didn't have a sudoku."

"No?"

"No."

"I'm wondering if that's because you happened to be at the crime scene."

"Why, Harvey Beerbaum, are you suggesting I arrived at this crime scene ahead of Chief Harper and removed a sudoku that could have shed light on the murder?"

"I'm not suggesting that. I'm asking if you did."

"Hang on, Harvey. I would have to ask

123

my lawyer here if there's a difference between suggesting and asking."

Becky smiled over her teacup. "If you think I'm getting in the middle of two cruciverbalists, you've got another think coming."

"Just what the hell does that mean?" Cora said. "Another think coming? When do you hear that in conversation? 'Hold on a minute, I have a think coming.'"

"It's another way of saying think again," Harvey said.

"You're wrong, you moron," Cora said.

Harvey's mouth fell open. "What?"

"Oh, not you, Harvey," Cora said. "You're wrong, you moron. It's another way of saying think again."

"Yes." Harvey cleared his throat. "We seem to have gotten off the subject. The sudoku at the crime scene?"

"Harvey," Cora said. "Let me stop you right here. I did not remove a sudoku from the crime scene. Chief Harper showed me the puzzle, but since I have *never* removed a sudoku from the crime scene, I didn't know what to tell him. And I don't know what to tell you, either."

"You think this new puzzle will shed some light on it."

"Absolutely not," Becky said adamantly.

Harvey looked at her in surprise. "Why do you say that?"

"Because it wasn't found at the crime scene. It's another matter entirely."

"I'm thinking maybe I should tell Chief Harper about this."

"Well, if it were connected to the crime, I could understand that. But it's not. It's totally unrelated, came from a different source."

"Look, Harvey," Cora said. "If you solve the puzzle and it says, 'I killed the guy at the crime scene,' then I'd have to concede the puzzles are related. But I bet you a nickel it doesn't. So there's no reason to spread it around."

"That depends on what it says."

"It certainly does, Harvey. Let's see what that is."

Cora shoved the puzzle in front of him.

Harvey picked up a pen, started on the puzzle.

"You do it in pen?" Cora said.

"Sure. Don't you? Oh, that's right."

The puzzle was simple. Harvey was done in minutes, without, Cora noted, crossing anything out.

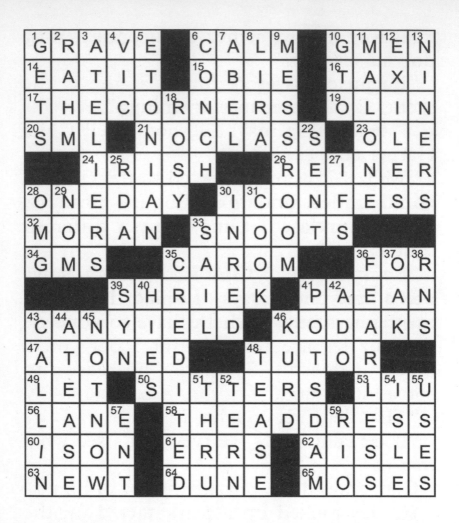

1 G	2 R	3 A	4 V	5 E	■	6 C	7 A	8 L	9 M	■	10 G	11 M	12 E	13 N
14 E	A	T	I	T	■	15 O	B	I	E	■	16 T	A	X	I
17 T	H	E	C	O	18 R	N	E	R	S	■	19 O	L	I	N
20 S	M	L	■	21 N	O	C	L	A	S	22 S	■	23 O	L	E
■	■	24 I	25 R	I	S	H	■	■	26 R	E	27 I	N	E	R
28 O	29 N	E	D	A	Y	■	30 I	31 C	O	N	F	E	S	S
32 M	O	R	A	N	■	33 S	N	O	O	T	S	■	■	■
34 G	M	S	■	■	35 C	A	R	O	M	■	■	36 F	37 O	38 R
■	■	■	39 S	40 H	R	I	E	K	■	41 P	42 A	E	A	N
43 C	44 A	45 N	Y	I	E	L	D	■	46 K	O	D	A	K	S
47 A	T	O	N	E	D	■	■	48 T	U	T	O	R	■	■
49 L	E	T	■	50 S	I	51 T	52 T	E	R	S	■	53 L	54 I	55 U
56 L	A	N	57 E	■	58 T	H	E	A	D	D	59 R	E	S	S
60 I	S	O	N	■	61 E	R	R	S	■	62 A	I	S	L	E
63 N	E	W	T	■	64 D	U	N	E	■	65 M	O	S	E	S

"The corners, I confess. Can yield the address." Harvey frowned, shook his head. "Once again, this would appear to refer to a sudoku."

"I'm afraid so."

"But you don't have one."

"Sorry, Harvey."

Cora stood up.

Harvey's face fell. "Oh, stay. Have another

cup of tea. Don't you want to discuss the puzzle?"

"It's pretty straightforward, Harvey."

"But it doesn't mean anything. Not without something else."

"I quite agree. That's why we have to go find it."

"Where will you look?"

Cora smiled. "If I knew that, I wouldn't have to look. Relax, Harvey." She put her arm around Becky Baldwin. "Nancy Drew and I are going to go snooping. If we find another puzzle, we'll be back."

CHAPTER 21

Cora was in a good mood as Becky piloted the car away from Harvey Beerbaum's. "Like the way I sidestepped the sudoku question?"

"Is that what you call it?"

"I told him I did not remove a sudoku from the crime scene, that I never removed a sudoku from the crime scene. All perfectly true, and yet utterly misleading. I thought as a lawyer you'd appreciate that. It was the absolute truth. I could have made that statement under oath, and there would be no way to get me for perjury."

"I'm delighted for you," Becky said dryly. "Your other statement, however . . ."

"What other statement?"

"That you didn't have a sudoku to go with the second puzzle. That's an out-and-out lie."

Cora shook her head, pityingly. "Oh, Becky, if you'd ever been married you'd understand the use of an out-and-out lie. I didn't, by the way. I just shook my head and said, 'Sorry.' Which could have meant, 'Sorry, I don't have it,' 'Sorry, you can't see it,' or, 'Sorry, you're a pompous prig who's never going to get to second base.' "

"You let him get to first base?"

"Oh, good, you're awake. I like that in a driver. Becky, you've had a shock, you had too much to drink, and you lost ten grand. You gotta calm down, keep quiet, and let me work."

"Work on what?"

"Solve the sudoku, find out the location of the blackmail drop."

"What good will that do? We don't have the money."

"We've gotta get the money."

"Where? You happen to have ten grand lying around? It's a nightmare. I'm on the hook for ten grand because someone stole the first ten."

"Your client."

"Huh?"

"Your client. Not you. You're taking this personally. It's your client's money, not yours."

"I'm responsible."

"How can you be responsible? It was stolen from you."

"That's one way to look at it."

"What's another?"

"It was lost."

"Huh?"

"I gave it to you and you lost it."

"You gonna dangle me in front of your client? Say it's my fault?"

"Don't be silly. You're my agent. It's my fault for hiring you."

"Thanks a lot."

"You wanna solve the damn sudoku already?"

"Not in a moving car. You want me to shove a pencil though your leg?"

Becky pulled off the road and stopped.

"Where are we?"

"I don't know, but we're not in a gas station."

They were on the soft shoulder of the road under a stand of oak trees. On the other side of the road was an open meadow. There was not a house in sight.

Cora whipped out the sudoku, went to work.

Becky was decidedly nervous. "What if a police car pulls up?"

"You're trying to remember what you forgot."

"What does that mean?"

"You're a woman and you don't know that

130

one? You really are a babe in the woods."

"Shut up and solve the damn thing."

"You're the one who started talking."

Becky held her tongue, and Cora whizzed through the puzzle.

"Got it!"

7	3	6	2	4	9	8	5	1
9	4	8	1	6	5	3	2	7
2	1	5	8	7	3	6	9	4
4	6	2	5	1	8	7	3	9
3	8	7	9	2	4	5	1	6
1	5	9	6	3	7	2	4	8
8	2	4	7	5	1	9	6	3
5	7	1	3	9	6	4	8	2
6	9	3	4	8	2	1	7	5

Becky leaned over and looked.

Cora pointed. "The four corners are seven, one, six, and five."

"Which tells you what?"

"I haven't a clue."

"Come on. You're been studying the crossword puzzle. I thought you got a hint."

"You want a hint?"

"That's what I'm paying you for."

"Actually, you haven't paid me yet."

"I was generalizing."

"Get specific. When were you thinking of paying me?"

"You ask that now? I gotta come up with ten grand."

"Technically, your client does."

"It doesn't matter where it comes from. I gotta have it in hand by nine tonight."

"Maybe a little before then, if you wanna have time to make the drop."

"What time do you need it?"

"You expect me to do this?"

"Yes, I do."

"Why don't you do it yourself?"

"I can't afford to get caught with the money."

"But *I* can?"

"If you get caught, you have a lawyer. If I get caught, I *am* a lawyer. Huge difference."

"Fine. Say I'm going to do this. Where are you going to get the money?"

"That's my business. Your business is to figure out the drop site."

"What am I dropping off?"

"You're dropping off ten grand. Just because my client can't pay it doesn't mean I can't get it."

"You're getting it?"

"My client's getting it."

"Okay. You get the money, I'll figure out where to take it."

"Fine. I'll drop you off. You can wait in my office."

"The hell I will. My niece just had a baby. You drop me at the hospital."

"You saw the baby."

"There were complications. I wanna see it again."

"You have to work on the puzzle."

"I'll work on the puzzle. I can work on the puzzle at the hospital as well as any-where else."

"Yeah, but —"

"This is nonnegotiable. You want me to do this, you drop me at the hospital."

"Fine," Becky said. "But you will work on the puzzle?"

"Promise."

CHAPTER 22

Becky Baldwin watched Cora sail through the front door of the hospital. There wasn't a prayer she was going to work on the puzzle. She'd go straight up to Sherry's room to check on the baby. Never mind the fact she had a blackmail payment to make and she didn't even know the drop site. She was racing upstairs to see a kid she'd already seen, who wouldn't be doing anything different than the last time. She was taking time off in the middle of a blackmail complicated by a murder that Becky could ill afford to have her take.

Becky exhaled angrily, shook her head. Realized the person she was angriest at was herself. She wondered how much of her resentment was a knee-jerk reaction to the fact the baby in question had been fathered by her high school sweetheart, who had opted to marry Sherry Carter and not her, while her own matrimonial prospects had dwindled down to a precious none.

Becky skidded into a turn. She realized she was driving too fast, eased up on the gas. The change was negligible. The car continued to hurtle down the road.

Ten thousand dollars. The son of a bitch wanted another ten thousand dollars. After having presumably stolen the first ten. It just wasn't fair. She'd worked so hard to get where she was. Rejected offers from large law firms, because she wanted to be her own boss. She'd come to Bakerhaven, started her own practice, and made a go of it, starting from scratch. True, the fact she was the only game in town helped. Even so, there wasn't that much need for a lawyer in Bakerhaven. There wasn't that much work. There wasn't that much one could do without feeling one was padding it somehow, one was making things up, one was protecting clients from dangers that were not there.

The blackmail was there. It was real, it was immediate, it was happening. It was threatening to scuttle her practice. It wasn't just about making an illegal payment. It was about making it twice. It was like being blackmailed for being blackmailed. Talk about unfair. It wasn't like she'd lost the money. She'd just given it to Cora. However questionable that decision might seem now, it was a no-brainer then. She sure wasn't bringing it herself.

Becky screeched into a turn, headed out toward the mall. A silly precaution, still she couldn't help herself. The situation called for silly precautions.

The mall parking lot was crowded in front of Target and the Stop and Shop, less so in front of the other entrances. The one Becky wanted was around to the left. She circled the mall at way too great a speed, incurred the glare of a driver who would have been more forgiving had he been aware of the pulchritude of the person who cut him off. She pulled into a spot and was out the door while the car was still rocking.

Becky hurried to the mall entrance, wrenched the door open, slipped inside.

On the side was a pay phone, nearly an anachronism in Bakerhaven, a rare relic of days gone by.

Becky snatched up the receiver, dropped in a quarter, made the call.

One ring.

Two rings.

Three rings.

Finally the click of the phone being answered.

A voice said, "Yes?"

"I need more money."

CHAPTER 23

Cora Felton scooted in the front door of the hospital, flattened herself against the wall, and peered out cautiously through the glass door. She half expected to see Becky Baldwin watching to make sure she went inside. But, no, Becky was driving off.

Cora wrenched the door open, slipped out, and ran crouching to the parking lot. Her trusty Toyota was right where she had left it. She zapped the door, leaped inside, started it up, gunned the engine. She backed out of the spot, slammed the car into gear, and peeled out, cutting off an ambulance.

Becky had turned left. Cora was sure of it. She swerved out, skidded into a turn.

The road was long and straight. There were no cars in sight, but a dot up ahead looked promising. The Toyota hurtled down the road. The dot grew, gradually took the shape of a car. Cora eased up on the gas, tagged along behind.

What a horrible situation. It was a sad state of affairs when you couldn't trust your own lawyer. Even when you were doing illegal things for her. At least if you were committing a felony, you ought to be in on the game. But, oh, no. *Lawyer client privilege.* As if that were some sacred thing that couldn't be violated. Hell, she was a client, too. Didn't that count for anything?

And then when everything blew up in her face, when she stumbled over a corpse and the money went south, surely that would be the time to clue her in. But, oh, no, little Miss Lawyer-Pants gets up on her huffy high horse, and the facts aren't good enough for the hired help.

That was the whole problem right there. Cora wasn't being allowed to contribute her expertise, her knowledge, her logic, her deductive reasoning. No, she was being hired as a paid functionary carrying out a task. An illegal task, but that was somewhat incidental. In point of fact, it was a routine task being carried out for an unspecified reason. At least for a nonspecific reason.

Cora snorted. Even in her own thoughts she was editing her speech, from force of habit, to keep up the Puzzle Lady façade.

From her vantage point, two rows over, Cora watched Becky hop out of her car and head toward the mall. Could she be using the pay phone? Cora had done that on occasion, but then she didn't have a cell phone. Becky did. If she were using the pay phone, that was interesting indeed.

Cora waited until Becky went in, then crept up to the entrance, and peered through the window.

Sure enough, Becky was on the phone.

Cora bit her lip. There was no way to get close enough to listen in, not without letting Becky see her. Cora stayed put. She couldn't hear the conversation, but she could at least see where Becky went.

Becky came straight back at her.

Whoops.

Cora fell all over herself getting out of the way. She scrunched down, scurried back to her car, slipped into the driver's seat, and peered out over the steering wheel.

Becky was climbing into her car. She clearly hadn't seen her.

Cora followed Becky back to her office.

That told the story. Becky called the client, and the client had to scare up the money. Ten grand. That ought to take a while.

Cora turned around and drove back to the hospital

CHAPTER 24

Becky looked up as Cora came in. "You got the address?"

"You got the money?" Cora countered.

"Yes, I got the money. You know where to take it?"

"Yes, I do."

"Care to share that information?"

"I don't know why. No one's sharing anything with me."

"Are you an attorney? Do you have a client? Is there some reason you shouldn't tell me what you know? Particularly since I hired you to do so."

"Well, when you put it like that," Cora said. "Who wouldn't want to cooperate?" She took her cigarettes from her drawstring purse, tapped one out of the pack.

"Not in here," Becky said.

"Really?" Cora whipped out a lighter, lit up. "You kind of lost your leverage, didn't you? What with you telling me nothing and me having things you want to know." She leaned back in her chair, put her feet up on the desk, and blew a smoke ring. "Wanna hear how I doped out the drop site?"

Becky took a deep breath, exhaled slowly. Then she smiled and said sweetly, "I'd love to."

"Good. Give me the money."

"What?"

"Let's see the money."

"You want me to show you the money?"

"I certainly do. There's little point without the money."

"Don't worry. I'll have the money."

"You *don't* have the money?"

"I have the money. It's being delivered."

"It's coming by messenger?"

"That's right."

"Great. Let's give the messenger boy the coordinates and let *him* make the drop."

"Very funny. And what might those coordinates be?"

"Why do you need to know?"

"What?"

Cora shrugged. "If I'm making the drop, what's it to you?"

Becky took a deep breath. Then she turned, grabbed Cora's purse.

"Hey!" Cora said.

"If you're going to act like a child, I will

treat you like a child." Becky plunked the purse down on her desk, sat behind it. "Now, I'm the teacher and you're the bad student. You may have your purse back after class. Meanwhile, I'll keep it, so you won't light any more cigarettes. Or take out your gun and shoot me."

"Fine," Cora said. "Be that way." She leaned back, took an insolent drag.

"Now then, class," Becky said. "Who can tell me the site of the money drop?"

Cora put up her hand.

"Yes? Miss Felton?"

"Would you like me to go to the board?"

"The blackboard needs erasing," Becky said. "Couldn't you just recite from there?"

"The drop's in the cemetery."

That jolted Becky out of her teacher mode. "Huh?"

"It's in the cemetery, in front of a gravestone."

"How in the world did you get that?"

"The corner squares of the sudoku, clockwise from the upper right, are 1567. The words *oak* and *lane* are in the crossword puzzle. The address of the cemetery is 1567 Oak Lane."

Becky's mouth fell open. "What?"

"It's a perfectly logical conclusion." Cora blew another smoke ring. "It was also on the piece of paper I found under your door as I came in. I suppose that was a bit of a hint. Not that I'd have needed it, or anything."

"Piece of paper?"

"I'd show it to you, but it's in my purse."

Becky dug the paper out of Cora's purse, unfolded it and read, " 'Bakerhaven Cemetery, 1567 Oak Lane.' "

"Yeah. Nice deduction, huh? And there's directions. Four left, five right, or whatever. Must mean counting graves."

"Gotta be," Becky said. "And it gives you landmarks. Tomb of Jablowsky. Grave of Pinehurst."

"Just like MapQuest."

The phone rang.

Becky scooped it up. Had a brief conversation which consisted largely of her listening and occasionally saying, "Uh huh."

Finally she hung up the phone.

"What's up?"

"The money's here."

"I don't see it."

"I'm going to go get it. You stay here."

"I'm coming with you."

"No, you're not."

"Try and stop me."

"Cora, I got a delicate situation here. Don't screw it up."

Becky darted out the door.

Cora jumped up, grabbed her purse off the desk, and ran after her.

By the time Cora reached the door Becky was already at the bottom of the steps. She took the stairs two at a time. Halfway down she tripped and fell. She felt a jarring pain in her side, rolled over once, summersaulted to the bottom. She clambered to her feet. Nothing seemed broken. She plunged through the door.

Becky was running down the alley toward Main Street. Cora gave chase. She emerged from the alley just in time to see Becky climb into her car halfway down the block.

Cora's Toyota was parked in front of the library. She hurried across the street, fumbled in her purse for her keys.

She couldn't find them. That was odd. She could always find them. They were attached to an ornate key ring. Where the hell were they?

Down the street Becky gunned the motor and backed out of her head-in parking space. Damn. She was getting away, and —

Cora's mouth fell open.

Out of the driver's side window, Becky was dangling the keys she'd stolen from Cora's purse. Becky smiled and took off.

Cora was fit to be tied. This was *not* happening. Becky was *not* getting away.

Cora glanced around in frustration.

There were three cars parked in front of the library. One of them was Iris Cooper's. Cora remembered the first selectman often stopped off to pick up a book on her way home. She remembered something else, too.

Cora ran to the car, looked in the window. Sure enough, the keys were dangling from the ignition. Cora wrenched the door open, hopped in, started up the car. She backed out of the parking space, sped down the street.

Becky Baldwin had a good head start but she was heading north, and there weren't that many turnoffs heading north. South there was Post Road, and the fork just past old Colson's place. But north there wasn't a major intersection for over a mile.

Cora stomped on the gas, tested Iris Cooper's zero to sixty acceleration. For a station wagon, it wasn't bad. On the straightaway, Cora could see a car in the distance. She hoped it was Becky.

It was. As Cora narrowed the distance, she could see the shape of Becky's Honda just before it went around the turn. It looked like she was heading for the mall. Which made sense. If you're having a clandestine meeting you either want to have it where there's no one, or everyone. Becky had chosen everyone, hoping to blend in with the crowd. Fat chance, looking like that. Even conservatively dressed, she'd be lucky to pull it off. Of course it didn't matter if she was noticed, it only mattered if it was noticed who she was with.

Becky turned into the mall. For a moment Cora thought maybe she was going to make another phone call. But no, she went right on by that entrance and pulled up in front of Starbucks.

No fair. Cora had introduced Becky to Starbucks. And now she was using it as a rendezvous?

She wasn't.

Becky got out of her car, looked around. She walked over to a black rental car parked in the next row. She pulled open the passenger door and slid in.

Cora couldn't see who was in the driver's seat, but it didn't matter. She had him. It was just a question of how long she should let them talk. Not very long she figured. With her luck, Becky'd hop out and the car would drive off.

The hell with it. She wasn't manufacturing evidence for court. It didn't matter if the money had changed hands. She just wanted to know who it was.

Cora got out of her car, walked over to the rental, and wrenched open the passenger door.

Her timing was good. Becky had the fat envelope in her hand.

"Ah! Caught in the act!" Cora said. "Well, it serves you right. What a pain in the ass. Why couldn't you just *tell me* who the client was?"

Cora didn't wait for an answer. She pushed Becky back out of the way.

And stopped dead.

Sitting in the driver's seat was the last person in the world Cora ever expected to see.

Her ex-husband, Melvin.

CHAPTER 25

"What the hell are you doing here?"

Melvin smiled. "Hello, Cora."

"Don't hello Cora me. You sit there shoving blackmail money at a lawyer. At *my* lawyer. Who won't even tell me what's going on. That's a fine position to be in with your attorney, don't you think, thank you very much."

"You're welcome."

"Don't get cute with me. I'm not amused." Cora shook her head disbelievingly. "I might have known. Becky acting all weird on me, and nothing adding up. Who could possibly create that kind of chaos?"

"I think you give me too much credit."

"What the hell are you doing in Bakerhaven?"

"Becky is a very good lawyer."

"Yes, she is. And so are a thousand other lawyers in Manhattan law firms, which are much more convenient to a person who doesn't happen to live in Bakerhaven."

"It's a nice drive."

"It's a lovely drive, Melvin. I don't suppose you're here to see the scenery."

Becky said, "Cora, you don't understand."

"Oh, I understand, all right." Cora jerked her thumb. "Out."

"Huh?"

"You heard me. Get out of the car. I'm going to have a little talk with my ex-husband, and I don't need an interpreter."

"Sounds romantic," Melvin said.

"I'll deal with you in a minute. Come on, Becky. You got what you came for. Take the money and run."

"Cora," Becky protested.

Cora literally dragged her out of the car. It wasn't easy. Becky was as thin as a supermodel, but she was scrappy and tough, and didn't take kindly to being manhandled. The only thing that stopped her from making a fuss was the glint in Melvin's eye at the prospect of witnessing a catfight.

Cora hopped in and closed the door. On second thought, she locked it.

She turned to find Melvin grinning at her roguishly. The man had the charm of an aging matinee idol. His hair, which owed its fullness to every restoration product on the market, from creams to implants, fell over his forehead in a rakish curl. His eyes twinkled. His lips formed that familiar smug smile. Khaki pants, a dress shirt open at the neck, and a wide-lapelled leather jacket formed an outfit some women might find attractive. But Cora knew better. She wasn't about to fall for his charm.

"So," Cora said. "How come you're being blackmailed?"

"What makes you think I'm being black-mailed?"

"Just a wild guess," Cora said sarcastically. "That and the ten grand you gave Becky Baldwin."

"You think that's blackmail money?"

"No. I think Becky's a bookie and you're placing a bet."

"Come on, Cora. You know me. What would I ever pay a nickel for?"

"Something that would put you in jail."

"Good point."

"And a rather obvious one, I would think. The only thing I don't understand is why you would come all the way up here to have a lawyer handle it."

"Really?" Melvin grinned. "Have you *met* your lawyer?"

"Are you kidding me? It was only that? I bet there was no blackmail at all. I bet you made the whole thing up just to have an excuse to hire her."

"That would be horribly devious, wouldn't it?"

"It certainly would. Which is right up your alley."

"Except for being terribly stupid."

"How so?"

"Well, for one thing, it's convoluted as hell."

"What's your point?"

Melvin put up his hands. "Okay, some of my schemes are not exactly straightforward. But don't you think ten grand is too much to pay for a woman?"

"You admit paying the ten grand?"

"Paying is such an ugly word. I gave it to a friend."

"For a retainer?"

"Sure. Let's say for a retainer."

Cora sighed. "Melvin, talking to you is what gave me those migraine headaches you were always complaining about."

"Ah, the good old days. Still you have to admit ten grand is too much to pay just to make it look like I'm being blackmailed."

"Yes. But if you're the one making it look like you're being blackmailed, you'll be the one picking up the payment. So it won't cost you anything at all."

"You always were logical, Cora. What else

did I do in this phony blackmail scheme?"

Cora blinked. She sucked in her breath. "You killed a man. That's going far, even for you."

"Don't be silly. I didn't kill anyone."

"Then who's the man in the Dumpster?"

"How the hell should I know?"

"You know about the man in the Dumpster?"

"Everyone knows about the man in the Dumpster."

"What do you know about him?"

"He's dead, and he's in a Dumpster."

"You didn't kill him?"

"Of course not."

"Then who did?"

"How the hell should I know?"

"Melvin, this isn't like you. I mean it's like you to go to absurd lengths to interest an attractive woman, but when you start leaving corpses around . . ."

"I didn't leave him."

"So you say. I don't have to believe you." Cora cocked her head. "Where are you going to be?"

"What do you mean?"

"While I'm making the blackmail payment."

"Oh, *you're* making the blackmail payment?"

Cora gave him a dirty look. "You *know* what I mean. While I'm making the drop-off, where will you be hanging out?"

"With my attorney, I hope."

"You'll be there when I get back?"

"I don't know. When are you going?"

"You don't know?"

"I never was good at details."

"That's a rather large detail."

"I'm not sure I was ever told."

Cora looked down at the floorboards. "So, you here with your wife?"

"What wife?"

"Your current wife. Whoever that might be."

"I don't have a wife."

"I find that hard to believe."

"I've got ex-wives. I believe you fall into the category."

"It's a noble sisterhood. We have annual meetings."

"Yeah."

"You here with a girlfriend?"

"Why would I want a girlfriend to meet my lawyer?"

"Good point. So you left her home?"

Melvin grinned. "You're awful eager to determine my marital status."

"Don't get all conceited. The number of ex-wives you're paying alimony to is directly proportional to how soon you'll run out of money."

"Nice try. I'm not buying. You want to know if I'm seeing someone.

Well, that's silly. I'm always seeing someone. You want to know if there's anyone special."

"Is there?"

"You're asking?"

"You brought it up."

"The only special women in my life are you and my lawyer."

"How is that supposed to make me feel?"

"Honored?"

"Please."

"Flattered?"

Before Cora had a chance to answer, there was a knock on the window. It was Officer Dan Finley. He didn't look happy.

Cora wasn't pleased, either. She rolled down the window, snarled, "What do you want?"

"I want to be home in bed," Dan groused. "I been up all night. This is Sam Brogan's shift. He called in sick so I'm still at it and then I have to catch this."

"Not exactly what I meant," Cora said. "What do you want with *me?*"

"Oh. Well, I'm sorry about this, but you happen to be under arrest."

154

Her mouth fell open. "You're kidding. Harper's charging me with the murder?"

"Oh, no, nothing like that. No one thinks you're a killer."

"So what are you arresting me for?"

"Grand theft auto."

CHAPTER 26

Chief Harper was on the defensive, a rather unusual position for a police chief to be placed in with a suspect who'd been caught red-handed. "If you'll just calm down."

Iris Cooper, in first selectman mode, was being diplomatic. "This was all a huge misunderstanding."

"Well, that's magnanimous of you," Harper said dryly, "seeing as how you reported the car stolen."

"I'm willing to concede there have been mistakes all around."

"I'm not willing to concede anything," Cora said. "I am speaking only with your assurance that the charges have been dropped."

"Iris Cooper has withdrawn the complaint."

"It is my understanding the police can file a complaint of their own," Cora said.

"I have no intention of doing so," Harper

told her.

"And that's the assurance under which I'm willing to talk."

"Of course. Now, if you'll just sign the waivers regarding false arrest."

"I don't see any reason why I should," Cora said.

"I do. There was no malicious intent. Iris reported a car stolen. We began an investigation. The librarian's son remembered seeing you drive off in it. We tried to relay this information to Iris. She was not available. We were forced to act on her complaint. On the basis of Iris Cooper's charge and Jimmy Potter's eyewitness testimony, we had no recourse but to issue a warrant. The car was spotted at the mall, where you were subsequently arrested."

"I wasn't in the car."

"No. But you happened to have the keys to it in your purse. No doubt the person who stole it left them there."

"You shouldn't be sarcastic, Chief. It ruins your lovable image."

"I don't feel very lovable right now. I've got an unsolved homicide, and you're not being much help. Which is a euphemism for obstructing justice. It's almost as if you stole a car to try to distract my attention from how mixed up you are in the murder."

"Chief, do you know how paranoid that sounds?"

"I'm not saying you're paranoid."

"Not *me. You.* You see conspiracies everywhere."

"Funny you should say that." Harper turned to Iris Cooper. "You dropping the charges?"

"I already said so."

"Fine. Then, if you don't mind, I'd like to talk to Cora alone."

Iris looked from one to the other. She shook her head, turned, and walked out.

Harper turned back to Cora. "Is it true what Dan said?"

"What?"

"When he picked you up, you were in a car with your ex-husband?"

Cora had a few choice comments about policemen in general, Dan Finley in particular, and all ex-husbands, past, present, and future, with whom she might be associated.

"I'll take that as a yes," Harper said. "If that's true, it would certainly account for your strange behavior."

"Strange behavior? Are you saying I've been acting strangely?"

"Well, I wouldn't want to jump to conclusions. I suppose for you stealing cars and crashing crime scenes is fairly normal."

Cora didn't dignify that with a response.

"Is that why you were holding out on me?" Harper said. "Because of Melvin?"

"Don't be silly."

"I'm not being silly. I've seen you around Melvin. I know how you become."

"I don't 'become' anything."

"You clammed up at the crime scene and called your lawyer."

"I didn't know he was here."

"And yet you wound up in a car with him."

"I didn't know he was here *then*. I just found out."

"You just found out today?"

"I just found out five minutes before Dan Finley knocked on the damn window."

"You didn't know it was him when you stole the car?"

"I didn't steal the car."

"Sorry. When you borrowed Iris Cooper's car without telling her you'd done so."

"That's right."

"You didn't know he was here until you got in the car?"

"That's right."

"Then how did you wind up in the car?"

Cora exhaled. "Chief, you're going around in circles and asking irrelevant questions that have little to do with anything. I didn't know Melvin was here then. I don't know why he's here now. I didn't know he was here, I just ran into him. I got in the car to ask him why he was here. Before I had a chance to find out, I was arrested by Dan Finley, who can consider himself off my Christmas list."

"Uh huh. And how did Melvin get mixed up in the murder?"

Cora offered the opinion that Chief Harper's intelligence might compare unfavorably with that of a tree stump.

"Not an unlikely conclusion," Harper said. "Melvin's not from Bakerhaven. The corpse is not from Bakerhaven. And if I may say so, your ex-husband has a reputation for rather unsavory practices."

"You may *not* say so. One of those unsavory practices was marrying me. Which didn't result in murder. And if anything was ever going to, that would have been it."

"Well, in that case, you'd have been the perpetrator."

"I was kidding."

"So was I. The fact remains, in the current homicide, Melvin is as good a lead as I've got."

"So arrest him."

"I can't do that."

"You arrested me."

"Melvin hasn't stolen a car."

"Neither have I."

"Let's not go around again. I don't know if I'd arrest Melvin, but I'd certainly pick him up for questioning if I knew where he was."

Cora knew where Melvin was. She bit her lip.

Whether Chief Harper noticed or not was a moot point. At that moment Becky Baldwin burst into the room.

"Again?" Becky said. "You arrested her again?"

"Not for the murder," Cora said. "For grand theft auto."

"What?"

As Becky listened to the recitation of events, her scowl grew deeper and deeper. "So. Not only have you arrested my client on a spurious charge, but you proceeded to interrogate her outside the presence of her attorney."

"Oh, pooh," Chief Harper said. "The charge was dropped. She could have called you if she wanted. She just didn't bother."

"She shouldn't have to demand an attorney. One should be offered her. That's an elementary Miranda rule. Did you inform her she had the right to an attorney?"

"Dan Finley picked her up. I don't know

161

what he told her."

"A rather serious admission from a chief of police. You not only have no control over your deputies, you don't even know what they're doing."

"Save it for the jury," Harper said. "When you barged in here, I was asking Cora about her involvement with one Melvin Crabtree. Perhaps you could be of some help in that area."

Becky sucked in her breath. Then she smiled and said, "I certainly could. It is my pleasure to inform you that whatever dealings my client may have had with her ex-husband are clearly none of your damn business."

"If it's connected to a murder, it's my business."

"Well, then you have information I don't have, Chief. In what way is her ex-husband connected to a murder?"

"That's what I'd like to find out."

"Well, if you don't know, you have no business to inquire into her personal matters."

"I wasn't inquiring into her personal matters. I just want to question the gentleman. I was asking if she knew where he was."

"I don't think that's how you phrased it, Chief," Cora said. "Or I would have told you quite simply that I didn't. If I recall correctly, you were asking me what he was up to, and I was telling you I had no idea, I didn't even know he was in town. Only you didn't want to take that as an answer."

Becky shook her head deploringly. "I can see my client's already said too much. And you did nothing to discourage her."

"That's part of the Miranda rule I'm not up on. Failure to discourage suspect."

"I thought I wasn't a suspect."

"You're not. Never mind, I'll talk to your lawyer. Ms. Baldwin. Do you know where Melvin is?"

"No, I don't. Which is too bad, because I run my law office largely for the purpose of providing you with information. Unfortunately, I don't have any. So, if you don't mind, I'm going to get my client out of here before you decide to arrest her again."

CHAPTER 27

"You lied to Chief Harper," Cora said, as she followed Becky out the door.

"Don't be silly. Lawyers never lie to the police. They make statements of fact which subsequently turn out to be false."

"It's a little different," Cora said. "You told him you didn't know where Melvin was, when he's right in your office."

"That's an assumption on your part."

"A pretty good one, seeing as how that's where he said he'd be. He said a lot that I failed to communicate to Chief Harper. I may have even made statements of fact which may subsequently turn out to be false."

"Yes, well that wasn't one of them," Becky said, "unless you have information I don't have."

"Don't be silly. Melvin's your client. He's in your office. You can spin it any way you like, but that happens to be the case."

"Well, that will certainly make things easier. Let's go have a little talk with him, shall we?"

Becky led the way up the stairs, flung open the office door.

Cora pushed by her, stopped dead.

The office was empty.

"Where is he?" Cora asked.

"I have no idea. I know you find that concept hard to grasp. Just because you suspect everyone of lying doesn't mean some people aren't telling the truth."

"Melvin isn't here?"

"That's right."

"I don't believe it. How could you let him out of your sight?"

"I really have no control over the man."

"He's your client."

"He's not my client. He's not here. Deal with it."

Cora slumped into a chair, rubbed her forehead. "Oh, my God."

"What's the matter?"

"Don't you see what this does? I was going to make the drop. Melvin was going to stay with you. So if someone picks up the money it couldn't be Melvin."

"It isn't Melvin."

"There's no way to prove it now."

"I don't need you to prove it. I just need

you to do the job." Becky sat at her desk, shook her head. "What the hell do you mean stealing a car? If Iris Cooper hadn't withdrawn the complaint, you'd be in jail."

"I only stole a car because you stole my car keys."

"To keep you from following me. For all the good it did."

"Yeah. So I wouldn't find out your client was Melvin, which I found out anyway, which you're still trying to deny. Look, Becky, this whole lack of trust thing is getting us nowhere. Don't you realize I can be much more valuable to you if I know the game?"

"That's debatable. Right now I'm not even sure I can use you to make the drop."

Cora's face fell. "What are you talking about?"

"You keep getting arrested. You may not realize it, but that's one good way of calling attention to yourself. And this is not the type of thing you wanna hire a brass band."

Cora'd had enough. "Fine. You make the drop."

Becky's mouth fell open. "What?"

"I'm tired of being pushed around. If you're not happy, do it yourself."

"I can't do it myself."

"Then quit grousing and let's talk this

166

over. So, Melvin's your client."

"I'm not prepared to admit that."

"Well, *he* did."

"Huh?"

"You may have scruples, but Melvin doesn't. He says up front he's your client. He admits it's largely an attempt to get into your pants."

"Melvin said he's the client?"

"Of course he did. Kind of hard to deny after handing over the cash. On the other hand, he claims he doesn't know anything about the man in the Dumpster. That doesn't figure. After all, somebody's got to know him." Cora leaned back in her chair and lit a cigarette. "So you can see why I'm rapidly losing interest in this whole operation. As far as I was concerned, the only good thing about making the drop was Melvin would be in your office when I made it, so if anyone messed with the money it couldn't be him. Now that we've eliminated the possibility, there hardly seems much point."

"Tell it to the blackmailer."

"If there is a blackmailer. If it isn't all Melvin."

"Including the man in the Dumpster?"

Cora grimaced. "That's the whole thing. That's just not Melvin's style."

"Whereas blackmail is right up his alley?"

"Yeah, only he's much more suited as the blackmailer than the blackmailee."

"He's neither one."

"Gee, that has a familiar ring to it."

"What do you mean?"

"That's a statement of fact which, unfortunately, may later prove to be false."

"Yeah, yeah, fine. You gonna make the drop or not?"

"You're dorked if I don't. It's too late to get someone else."

"That's what comes of getting arrested. You run out of time."

"You don't have anyone else, do you? I've got you over a barrel. I'm not sure what that means. Though the thought of you spread-eagled on top of a barrel certainly has interesting connotations."

"I need you to do it. I can't get anyone else."

"And if I refused? Unless you told me who your client was?"

"I'd have to call your bluff. And we'd both sit here while the time ran out."

"That doesn't sound very satisfactory." Cora cocked her head. "You got the money?"

"You know I got the money."

"I'm not taking anything for granted. If

you got the money, I want to see it."

Becky opened her desk drawer, pulled out a manila envelope.

"You leave ten grand lying around in your desk?"

"No one knows it's here."

"Melvin knows it's here."

"Melvin's not going to take it."

Cora shook her head, pityingly. "And you kid me about him messing up my head."

"Fine. I don't want to argue about it. The point is, he didn't take it. The money is here."

"Open the envelope."

"It's sealed."

"I know it's sealed. I don't want it sealed."

"The money's there."

"You'll pardon me if I don't take your assurance. You're not the one running around in the dark with it. If I get shot over this, it damn well better be real."

"It's real."

"I'll be the judge of that."

Becky glared at Cora. Exhaled. Picked up the manila envelope. She took out a letter opener, inserted it under the flap.

"Don't be a dope," Cora said. She snatched the envelope, ripped it open. "It's a plain envelope. You rip it up, you use a new one."

"If I've got a new one."

"It's a law office. You've got a new one."

Cora dumped the money out on the desk. It was two packets of bills, tied with rubber bands. She picked one up, looked. "Hmm. Hundreds."

"So?"

"I thought they wanted small, unmarked bills."

"They're unmarked."

"They're hundreds."

"Yes, they are."

"That's not small."

"It's the best I can do."

"It's not wise to cross a blackmailer."

"You're right," Becky said. "Could you change these for me before you drop them off?"

"No, I couldn't. I'm just pointing out, you're asked to bring one thing, you're bringing something else. Only you're not bringing it, you're making *me* bring it. It's a rather uncomfortable position to be in. When I'm dealing with a blackmailer, I like to be careful not to piss him off."

"You're not meeting the blackmailer."

"Yeah, but what if from his vantage point, the blackmailer watching me make the drop says, 'Wow, that's not big enough to hold ten grand. Think I'll kill the bitch.' "

"Then you shoot the blackmailer dead."

"What?"

"No one can blame you because it's legitimate self-defense."

"Running around the cemetery in the dead of night with ten grand in my pocket?"

"You got lost on your way to the bank."

Cora looked at her sharply. "Becky, what's up? This is not like you. You don't sound like yourself. You know what you sound like? You sound like me. It's like doing something illegal has blown every fuse in your nervous system and made you a little loopy. You know what your problem is? You're a small-town lawyer. You haven't had enough guilty clients. If you worked for a big Manhattan firm with clients in organized crime, you'd do stuff like this and think nothing of it. Hell, you'd be doing worse stuff than this if the client was an investment bank."

Becky took a breath. "All right, Cora. Look. I got a situation here. I'm doing the best I can. You wanna help me or not?"

Cora studied Becky's face. The young lawyer was clearly troubled. She chucked her on the arm. "Don't worry, kid. I got your back."

CHAPTER 28

The cemetery gate was closed. Cora had forgotten it would be. It had been some time since she'd been there. After dark you had to go over the wall.

Cora didn't want to go over the wall. She wasn't dressed for it. For climbing a stone wall she wanted to be wearing jeans or sweatpants, not hiking her skirt up and scratching her bare legs over rough stone. But there was no help for it. Cora didn't want to be the first woman in the world to run home and change in the middle of a blackmail payment.

Cora put her hands on the top on the wall, hopped, pushed, and managed to get waist-high to the top. She rolled onto her stomach and threw her legs over the other side.

And came down in a heap.

Great. If the blackmailer saw her, he'd think he was blackmailing a klutz.

That started a funny train of thought. Did

the blackmailer know who the client was? He must know it wasn't Becky. But did he know it wasn't her?

No, that made no sense. How could the blackmailer know something that could ruin you, and not know who you are?

So the blackmailer would know she was a paid functionary. He just didn't have to know what a low-level, ill-informed lackey she was. He must think she knew something. After all, she had a reputation. She was the goddamned Puzzle Lady. He would not expect her to be clueless.

She wasn't clueless. She had directions. She knew exactly where she was going.

Of course, that was starting from the main gate. Not from lying sprawled out at the bottom of the wall.

Cora brushed herself off, made her way through the dark over to the main gate. It didn't take bumping into too many gravestones for her to realize she should have brought a flashlight. How was she to know there would be no moon, and it would be a cloudy, starless night?

Cora reached the gate. She leaned against it, fumbled in her purse for her directions. She hoped she could *see* her directions. She had her lighter, but those things always ran out on you when you most needed them, and —

The gate swung open and Cora went over on her back.

She sprang to her feet, furious.

Unlocked? The gate was unlocked? Nonsense. The gate was never unlocked. It had a huge, iron lock, right in the middle. They always locked it.

Cora frowned. Or was she wrong about that? Was it actually a chain and padlock? It had been a long time, and she couldn't remember.

Was she getting old?

Cora took out the directions, careful not to lean on the gate again. She spun the dial on the lighter. It took two times to catch, not a good sign.

" 'Proceed straight up the road, turn left at the tomb of Jablowsky.' "

Cora snorted in disgust. Well, that was great. They couldn't tell you how far? There you were, flicking your Bic at every gravestone on the path.

On the other hand, *tomb* sounded more substantial than your ordinary, run-of-the-mill grave. She could skip the smaller stones. She could always come back to them. Assuming she had time.

Cora looked at her watch. Of course, she

couldn't see it. She spun the wheel on the cigarette lighter. Again, it took two spins.

So. Eight forty-five. She had fifteen minutes. Enough time, if she knew where she was going. Not enough time to get lost. She should have come here by daylight, plotted the course. She would have, if she hadn't been out getting arrested.

Cora hurried along.

Tomb?

Tomb?

Tomb?

Nothing she was passing could have qualified as a tomb.

She shone her light on a phallic-shaped obelisk, but that wasn't it.

In the distance, a dark form loomed large. At least relatively large.

It was square-shaped, not taller than she was. Could this be it? It was. The front of the square had a locked iron door with the inscription, MALCOLM JABLOWSKY. Cora wondered if he was in.

She turned left, started counting graves. She reached twelve, but were they counting that small one slightly out of line? That would certainly make a difference. If she miscounted, she would be in the wrong row.

But only one row off, she told herself.

Only there the problem multiplied. Seven-

175

teen up in this row might not be the same distance as seventeen up in the other. You got a few gaps in the line and it throws off your count. If you're wrong about one, you're wrong about the other.

Six, Cora counted. Six is really five, because the one out of line doesn't count. If I'm wrong, no one dies. Just someone's reputation.

Consoled, Cora plunged ahead.

Cora checked the directions. It wasn't seventeen up. It was only nine. Then right, and four graves to Pinehurst. That was good in that she could check the name on the grave. On the other hand, by turning right, she was going back in the direction from whence she'd come. Granted, nine graves higher, even so it was annoying.

The lighter flickered and went out. Cora wondered if that was just the wind, or if the damn thing had just run out of gas. She was torn between flicking it again to see, and not wanting to waste it.

Instead, she wasted several seconds while her eyes became accustomed to the dark. She could vaguely see the outline of the graves. She forged ahead, counting gravestones. At least going north, the gravestones were coming at her, and she was counting them head-on, an easier task than approaching from the side.

As Cora got nearer and nearer her blood began to race. The last time she'd been in the graveyard, a girl had been found murdered there. That seemed so long ago. And yet that sort of memory doesn't fade. Even dulled by the fact Cora had still been drinking at the time, the memory was clear as day. Cora wasn't eager to reach her goal.

Eight.

Nine.

Her ninth grave.

No need to consult the directions. To use up what was left of her lighter. Four graves to the right. Pinehurst. If the name was on the stone she was there.

Cora counted carefully, not wanting to blow it, not wanting to miss some grave slightly out of line.

She reached the fourth grave. There appeared to be no dark form on the ground.

Of course this might not be it. She had to risk the lighter.

She raised it.

Flicked it.

Once.

Twice.

Third time's the charm.

A spark ignited the flame.

There on the stone was the name Edward

Pinehurst.

Shielding the lighter from the wind, Cora moved it down the gravestone toward the ground.

There was no girl's body lying there.

Instead there were two sheets of paper.

A crossword puzzle and a sudoku.

Across

1 Enthusiastic to the max
5 Tabloids couple
9 Dull as dishwater
14 #2, famously
15 1953 Mel Ferrer musical
16 Essential acid type
17 Start of the hint

19 On the lam
20 Very recently
21 Scouts seek them
23 Upholstered couch
25 Fighter in gray
26 Port-__ cheese
30 Part 2 of the hint
35 Set in order
37 Rock's ZZ Top, e.g.
38 Prepare to drag race
39 Seine feeder
40 Cooling down
42 Raise the roof
43 Sushi roll topper
44 Basics
45 Parents' hiree
47 Part 3 of the hint
50 Stopwatch button
51 With 68-Across, how corners yield hint
52 "Eh"
54 Some athletic wear
58 Chanted words
63 IRA-establishing legislation
64 End of the hint
66 Pep up
67 In the thick of
68 See 51-Across
69 Looks from Groucho
70 Stage award
71 Gaelic tongue

Down

1 Greek earth goddess
2 Gung-ho
3 Billion: Prefix
4 Hardly ruddy
5 Volunteer's offer
6 Close with a suture
7 December helper
8 Oven accessory
9 California's "City of Opportunity"
10 Lab slide critter
11 Subatomic bit
12 Technical sch.
13 Is sufficient
18 Take a bite of
22 Pieces in the game Risk
24 Many loft dwellers
26 Sound from the bull pen
27 Grade school quintet
28 Type of pointer
29 Beehive State Indian
31 Tolkien beast
32 Headaches for a 45-Across
33 Flood zone sight
34 For all to see
36 Insignificant one
41 ATM-making co.
42 Tpk. or hwy.
44 Incas, e.g.

46 O. Henry technique
48 Egyptian president before Sadat
49 Pinpoint, with "on"
53 "Arf!" utterer in comics
54 Take form
55 Toledo's lake
56 Tear apart
57 Whack hard
59 Fundraiser gift, perhaps
60 German coal region
61 Gets mellower
62 A handful
65 Coverage co.

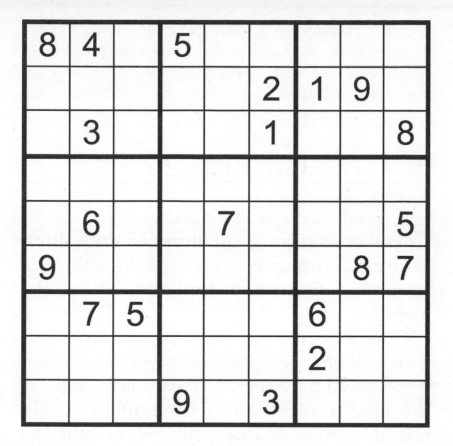

CHAPTER 29

Cora was so startled she dropped the lighter, plunging the grave into darkness, as a stream of frustrated expletives filled the night.

What a horrible turn of events. Here was a crossword puzzle she couldn't solve, even if she could have seen it. This was something the blackmailer hadn't thought of, could not have possibly foreseen. He thought she was a competent cruciverbalist, who ate crossword puzzles for breakfast and was smart enough to bring a flashlight. Well, wrong on both counts, buddy. Your blackmail scheme has just hit a big, fat snag.

Except for the payoff. Cora was making the payoff. Whatever else the blackmailer wanted her to do would have to wait.

Cora folded the pages, shoved them into her floppy, drawstring purse. She pulled out the blackmail money. She had to smile in spite of herself. She'd been so afraid the blackmailer would be able to tell the envelope wasn't big enough to hold ten thousand dollars in small unmarked bills. There wasn't a chance the guy could see a thing.

Cora set the envelope on the grave, propped it up against the gravestone.

And got the hell out of there.

All right, what was it? Four back? Nine down?

Who cares? She didn't have to follow the same path. She was looking for the main gate. She got her bearings, set off for it.

It was fairly easy going, except for barking her shins on gravestones. She reached the gate in minutes. Now, over the wall? No, the gate's open. Unless it was locked. If it was locked now, she was going to be pissed. It wasn't. She pushed against it and it swung open. She slipped out, pushed it closed. Hurried to the road. The car was right where she left it. She hopped in, drove off.

Things were not going well. That was an understatement. Becky was going to be pissed. Chief Harper was going to be pissed. The whole world was going to be pissed.

Cora slowed down as she hit the center of town. What now? Go see Becky Baldwin? With an unsolved puzzle? Not likely.

Cora drove straight to the hospital. She parked, went inside. Visiting hours were over. Cora assured the woman at the front desk she knew that, she wasn't visiting. While the woman was thinking that over, Cora hopped in an elevator, went upstairs.

Sherry was alone in the room. She was lying in bed with her head on the pillow. She was quiet, peaceful. Cora hated to disturb her.

Damn.

Cora flopped into the chair, reached in her purse, pulled out the crossword puzzle. If it wasn't too difficult, maybe she could solve it herself.

It looked like Sanskrit.

Which was silly. Some of the clues sounded pretty easy. And then she looked from the clue to the grid, and the answer she had thought of always had the wrong number of letters. Who were the people who actually solved these thing? Freaks, that's what they were.

"Cora?"

Sherry's eyes were open.

"Hi, kid. How are you?"

"I have a baby."

"Yeah. Isn't she wonderful?"

"Yeah."

"Where's Aaron?"

"They kicked him out. It's after hours." Sherry's eyes widened. "Hey, what are *you*

186

doing here?"

"Oh."

"What you got there?"

"It's a puzzle."

"Gimme."

"You sure?"

"Come on. Come on. I'm going stir-crazy. Give me the puzzle."

Cora passed it over.

"Where did you get this?"

"A blackmailer left it by a gravestone."

"Are you kidding me?"

"I wish I were."

"How bad is it?"

"I'm afraid it's telling me to do something I didn't know to do."

"What will happen then?"

"I have no idea. Becky won't tell me a damn thing. She won't even tell me who the client is. Even though I know."

"Who is it?"

"Melvin."

"He's here?"

"Yeah."

Sherry's pencil was flying over the puzzle. She looked up. "That doesn't make any sense. Who could blackmail Melvin?"

"I don't know. But he put up ten grand to keep them from doing it. I left it by the gravestone. I'm hoping these puzzles don't say that was the wrong thing to do."

"Aha."

"*Aha?* What do you mean by *aha?*"

Sherry grimaced. "You're not going to like this."

"Why? What does it say?"

"Did a sudoku come with this?"

"Oh, don't tell me." Cora snatched the puzzle from Sherry, read the theme entry.

" 'Eight left from Jablo. Turn north when you go.' "

"What's Jablo?"

"There's a tomb of someone named Jablowsky in the cemetery."

"Well, that's pretty straightforward."

"Yeah. Why did you think there was a sudoku?"

"Oh. Look at 51-Across."

Cora read, " 'With 68-Across, how corners yield hint.' And the answers are 'add' and 'them'."

"Is there a sudoku?"

"Yes."

"Did you solve it?"

"No."

"Better do it."

Cora took the pencil back from Sherry, whipped out the sudoku, sat down, and started solving it.

"Damn."

"What?"

"It's challenging."

"You can't do it?"

"Of course I can. It's just difficult. I have to think harder and it will take longer."

"What's it say?"

"I'm still working."

"Did you get the corners?"

"Be quiet."

"You don't have to solve the whole thing, just the corners."

"If you weren't here in the hospital, I'd put you in one."

"If you just had the corners, you don't need the rest."

"Will you shut up?"

"See?" Sherry said. "Now you know how I feel when I'm trying to solve a crossword puzzle."

"In a moment you're going to know how you feel when you try to *eat* a crossword puzzle."

"That's right. Attack a poor, defenseless mother."

"I don't believe it. You're playing the mom card already? I warn you, it has a limited number of uses. You use 'em up, you're out of luck."

"That's what you think. The mom card is forever."

"Will you shut up? You made me write a five instead of a seven."

"Is that bad?"

"Oh, you're really being naughty." Cora filled in the last number. "And . . . done!"

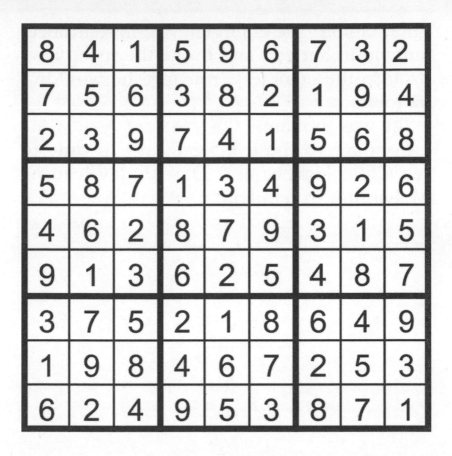

8	4	1	5	9	6	7	3	2
7	5	6	3	8	2	1	9	4
2	3	9	7	4	1	5	6	8
5	8	7	1	3	4	9	2	6
4	6	2	8	7	9	3	1	5
9	1	3	6	2	5	4	8	7
3	7	5	2	1	8	6	4	9
1	9	8	4	6	7	2	5	3
6	2	4	9	5	3	8	7	1

Cora looked at the sudoku. "Okay, the four corners add up to seventeen. Seventeen graves north of the tomb."

A nurse stuck her head in the door. "Hey, you can't be in here."

"It's all right, I'm not," Cora said, and pushed by her out the door.

Cora ran down the corridor, right by the empty nurses' station. She couldn't wait for the elevator. She took the stairs two at a time, ran out the emergency room entrance, jumped in her car, and broke the speed laws back to the cemetery, praying she wouldn't be too late.

She was too late.

Cora got to the front gate just in time to see Chief Harper and Dan Finley leading Melvin out in handcuffs.

CHAPTER 30

Cora skidded to a stop, blocking the police cruiser. She hopped out of her car, strode up to Chief Harper.

"What the hell is going on here?"

"We just arrested your ex-husband."

"What for?"

"Murder."

"Who's dead?"

"That's what we'd like to know."

"Don't piss me off, Chief. I've got a short fuse on this one."

"Cora, shut up," Melvin said. "I can take care of myself."

She eyed him witheringly. Even in handcuffs he looked haughty, brash, the cock of the walk. "Oh, sure. What a big boy you are."

"I'm not supposed to talk. They say I've got a right to an attorney. I hope that cute blond one's available."

Cora exhaled angrily. "I don't know which of you is more annoying. Chief, you wanna let me in on what's happening here, or do I have to go postal?"

"That's a rather prejudicial remark. I think Miss Blakely would take exception to it."

Cora made a comment the postmistress, Miss Blakely, would almost certainly take exception to.

"There's my little spitfire!" Melvin said.

Cora ignored him, stared down the chief. "Come on. What the hell happened?"

"We had a phone call. Report of shots fired in the cemetery."

"Shots!"

"That's right, shots," Melvin said. "So you go out and arrest an unarmed man."

"Anyone can throw away a gun," Harper said.

"What shots? What gun?" Cora demanded. "When did this happen?"

"Must have been twenty minutes ago."

"Twenty minutes?"

"See how stupid that is?" Melvin said.

Cora looked at him sharply, but his face was angelic. For Melvin.

"Who made the complaint?"

"It was a phone call."

"An anonymous phone call?"

"The person didn't give a name."

"See?" Melvin said. "It just gets worse and

worse. My attorney's going to have a field day."

"Fine," Harper said. "And you can call your attorney. Just as soon as Dan gets you down to the station and gets you booked."

"What's he charged with?" Cora said.

"I'm not charged with anything, because I didn't *do* anything."

"He's charged with trespass and illegal entry."

"Oh, give me a break."

"He was tiptoeing around the cemetery after dark with ten thousand dollars in his pocket, and he won't say why. Now, I'm not claiming he shot someone and took it. On the other hand, it would seem a poor time to be getting belligerent."

Cora gave Melvin a look.

He smiled, shrugged his shoulders. "Chump change. Tell 'em what I used to carry in Vegas."

"Wanna move your car so Dan can take him down to the station?"

"You're not going?"

"I gotta follow up on that report of shots fired."

"Sure thing."

Cora hopped in her car, backed up, pulled off to the side.

Dan Finley backed the cruiser out of the

drive, turned around, headed back toward town.

Cora didn't follow. She walked over to where Chief Harper was getting a flashlight out of his car.

"You going with your husband?"

"He's not my husband."

"Your ex-husband. Aren't you going with him? Or are you more interested in prowling around the cemetery?"

"I wasn't until you said shots fired."

Chief Harper looked at her, cocked his head. "You got your gun in your purse?"

"You know I do."

"Can I see it?"

"It hasn't been fired, Chief."

"Then you won't mind me making sure."

Cora dug in her drawstring purse, handed him the gun.

He sniffed it, handed it back.

"Now you know I didn't fire those shots, you mind if I help you find who did?"

"Be my guest."

"You got a flashlight?"

"You didn't bring one?" Harper asked.

"Why would I bring one?"

"I don't know. Why are you here?"

"Are you kidding me?" Cora said. "Report of shots fired."

"You didn't *know* there were shots fired."

"That's what I told *Melvin*. If you wanna go by what I told Melvin . . ."

"Are you saying you *did* know there were shots fired?"

"I'm not making any statements until I know what the facts are. That would be pretty stupid. What do you say we check this out?"

"What do you say we do? And if it doesn't check out, you and I are going to have a little talk."

Harper popped the trunk, took out a second flashlight, gave it to Cora. "Come on."

"Where are you going?"

"We gotta go over the wall."

"You can go over the wall, Chief. I'm going in the gate."

"The gate's locked."

"I don't think so."

"What?"

"Don't they lock it with a chain? It's been a while, but isn't that the way it works?"

Harper gave her a look. He walked up to the gate. Pushed on it. It swung open.

"That's a break," Cora said. "I'm not really wearing climbing gear. Okay, where do we look?"

Harper pointed off to the right. "That way."

"How come?"

"That's where Dan saw Melvin moving."

"He saw him moving?"

"His light."

"Oh. Didn't Dan already search there?"

Harper shook his head. "Huh uh. Melvin was coming this way. Dan didn't want him to run. He waited for him to come out."

"When did he arrest him?"

"When he came over the wall."

"How come you don't have Sam?"

"Don't need him. So far it's just shots fired. Dan caught it, checked it out. Saw the light moving and called me. I showed up right after he made the arrest."

"Nobody lives around here, Chief."

"What's your point?"

"Who's gonna hear shots fired?"

"So far it's just a theory."

"So's the idea the shots came from the cemetery just because Melvin did. Melvin doesn't have a gun. I'll bet you he hasn't fired one."

"So?"

"You check to the right, I'll check to the left."

"Why?"

"There's no point in me looking where you're looking. We'll see the same thing."

Chief Harper set off in the direction she'd

indicated.

Cora set out at a similar angle to the left. She was swinging the flashlight in a wide arc. This allowed her to scan a greater path in front of her. It also allowed her to change the angle slightly within the arc, and head back to the right. After a while, the flashlight picked up the tomb at the outer limit of the arc.

Chief Harper was just a bobbing light in the distance. Cora continued to swing her light in a leftward arc, while inching her way to the right.

Finally she reached the tomb.

Okay, with this as a starting point, eight graves to the left. It was a lot easier counting them with a flashlight than with a lighter. Now seventeen north, the sum of the four corners of the sudoku.

Cora counted the gravestones, her mind racing a mile a minute. Melvin. Why did it have to be Melvin? She could handle anything but Melvin. A conceited, obnoxious, meddling son of a bitch. He hadn't fired a gun. She *knew* he hadn't fired a gun, because she was *in* the cemetery twenty minutes ago when that call came in. She was damn lucky she missed Dan Finley. She must have left just before he got there. But she must have been there when the shots were fired, so Melvin didn't fire them, there were no shots, but what the hell was that son of a bitch doing in the arms of the police clutching her damn ten grand? Which was his ten grand to begin with, so was this all just a wild-goose chase to give him a chance to play games with Becky Baldwin? If it was, the next time Chief Harper sniffed her gun it would have been fired. Six times. At close range.

She was almost there. Just two more graves. Unless she'd miscounted. Which would have been easy with so many thoughts jumbling through her head. Well, what did she expect to find? Melvin had appropriated the money. In point of fact, there should be absolutely nothing. Just a bare grave. Unless there was another puzzle there, sending her somewhere else. If there was, she was going to freak out. She couldn't solve it, so she couldn't let Chief Harper know about it, so she'd have to appropriate it, and carry it around with her for as many hours as it took to straighten out the mess that Melvin had created by getting nabbed by the cops. Which wasn't entirely his fault, unless *he'd* phoned in the report of shots fired. But that was too convoluted even for Melvin, wasn't it? Maybe not. She knew for a fact now he'd given Becky the money and stolen it back.

Damn it, was that the first grave or the second? The second, definitely the second. That's the first grave, and —

Cora stopped and stared.

A young woman was stretched out in front of the gravestone.

She was clearly dead.

CHAPTER 31

The cemetery was lit up like a Christmas tree. First there were the police lights, which Officer Sam Brogan had set up in a semi-circle around the crime scene. Sam had balanced them on the tops of gravestones, which probably wouldn't have pleased the relatives of the dear departed any, if they got wind of it.

Then there were the floodlights from the Channel 8 news van parked just outside the cemetery gate. They had tried to park *inside* the cemetery gate, but Sam Brogan put a stop to that, stringing a crime scene ribbon straight across the cemetery entrance.

Of course, that was where Rick Reed set up for his shot.

"Murder in Bakerhaven," Rick began triumphantly. "And, in a bizarre twist, this time the murder is an eerie carbon copy of a murder that took place in Bakerhaven years ago. In both cases, a young girl was found dead in front of a grave."

The camera pulled back as Rick Reed pointed his microphone at Cora Felton, standing next to him.

"I am talking to Bakerhaven's own Cora Felton, the Puzzle Lady, who has assisted the police on numerous occasions, and who was involved in that original case. Miss Felton, is it true that this is the second time you've found a young girl's body in the cemetery?"

Cora smiled sweetly. "No, it's not true."

Rick stopped in mid follow-up question. "Really? But I was told you did."

"Better check your source, Rick. I've never found a young girl in the cemetery before."

Rick frowned. "But the first case, years ago. Wasn't a young girl found in front of a grave?"

"Yes, but not by me. I never heard of that case until much later."

The young reporter, clueless under the best of circumstances, floundered helplessly. "But it's true you solved the case?"

Cora smiled. "I think Chief Harper would take exception to that, Rick. I was there while the police solved the case, but I sure didn't do it for them."

"Oh. Well, in this case, is it true you found the body?"

"Yes, it is."

"Well, that's something," Rick said. "You found the body. And what were you looking for?"

"A body."

"You were looking for a body?"

"Absolutely."

"How did you know a body was there?"

"I didn't. The police got a report of shots fired. When shots are fired, you have to wonder what they hit. Sometimes it's a person."

"What made you think it was in this case?"

"I didn't think it was in this case."

"Then why were you looking for a body?"

"To see if there was a body. I was hoping there wasn't."

"But there was."

"Yes."

"How did you come to find it?"

"Trial and error."

"I understand you and Chief Harper were both looking for a body."

"I'm glad you understand."

"But you found it. How did you beat him to it?"

"I didn't beat him to it. He was looking in one half of the cemetery. I was looking in the other. The body happened to be in my half."

Sherry Carter, watching the interview on the small hospital TV in her room, made as if to push Aaron Grant off the bed. "Will you get out of here?"

"I don't have to go."

"Yes, you do. It's a murder. Cora's on TV giving interviews to Rick Reed."

"Yeah, and what's that all about?" Aaron said. "She usually avoids him like the plague."

"And you can't wait to find out why. You saw the baby. The baby's fine. The baby's asleep. You proved you're a good husband and father by sneaking in after visiting hours to see us, now get the hell out."

"But —"

"Go."

Aaron got up, leaned down and kissed her, and hurried out the door.

Aaron got to the cemetery just in time to see the EMS van leaving with the body, followed closely by Dr. Barney Nathan's car. Aaron parked behind the Channel 8 news van. As he got out of his car, Cora came up to meet him.

"Hi, Aaron. What kept you?"

"I didn't want to leave Sherry."

"I thought you went home."

"I came back."

"She okay with you leaving again?"

"She threw me out of the room."

Cora nodded. "That's a good sign."

"What happened?"

"You see my interview?"

"Yeah. You didn't say anything."

"Well, I was talking to Rick Reed."

"Why?"

"Harper asked me to."

"And you always do everything he wants."

Cora grimaced. "I found the body. He asked me if I'd like to answer his questions or Rick Reed's. Frankly, it was a toss-up."

"Anything irregular with you finding the body?"

"Not that you could put in the paper."

"What *can* I put in the paper?"

"The body's a young woman. Probably thirty. Probably shot."

"Who was she?"

"No one knows. There was no identification on the body."

"Just like the man?"

"In that respect."

"You have no idea what she was doing there?"

"She was lying there dead."

"Come on, Cora."

"There was no reason for her to be there. There was no reason for a man to be in the Dumpster."

"Was there a reason for you to be there?"

"Don't be a wise-ass. No one likes a wise-ass."

"I'm serious."

"I know you are. So is Chief Harper. Which is why I'm answering Rick Reed's questions instead of his."

"Why isn't Becky protecting you?"

"Becky's a little busy right now."

"Oh?"

"My ex-husband Melvin's in town. Dan Finley arrested him just before I found the body."

Aaron's mouth fell open. "Arrested him? Where?"

"In the cemetery."

"Melvin was in the cemetery?"

"That's right."

"You didn't mention that to Rick Reed."

"No kidding."

"Is that why you did the interview?"

"It's one reason. There was a report of shots fired in the cemetery. Dan, investigating, found Melvin in the cemetery."

"Is that all?"

"That's not enough?"

"What aren't you telling me?"

"I'm telling you a lot more than I told Rick Reed. He doesn't even know about Melvin. Which means Dan Finley hasn't

207

tipped him off. You know Dan will as soon as they come up with a charge that will stick."

"He arrested him on no charge?"

"He arrested him on suspicion of discharging a firearm within town limits."

"You're kidding."

Cora shook her head. "No, apparently the cemetery falls within Bakerhaven township."

"Melvin had a gun?"

"No."

"That should make the charge less valid."

"Shots were fired in the cemetery. Melvin was found in the cemetery, and won't explain why he was there."

"You were also found in the cemetery?"

"Yeah."

"Chief Harper sniff your gun?"

"He always sniffs my gun. The man has a fetish."

"I can see why you opted for Rick Reed."

"I gotta talk to the chief sooner or later. I just opted for later."

Dan Finley drove up in his cruiser, hopped out, headed for the cemetery gate.

"Dan," Cora called. "Where's Melvin?"

"I left him with his lawyer."

"You let him out?"

"No, he's in the lockup."

"You gonna tell Rick Reed?"

"Now, you always think I do that."

"Because you always do. Can you hold off in this case?"

"How come?"

"The chief asked me to talk to Rick. I haven't mentioned Melvin, and I don't want Rick to."

"The chief asked you to talk?"

"I owed him a favor. I gave Rick an earful for him."

"What did you tell him?"

"Not a damn thing. And I wanna keep it that way. Don't tip him off until the chief spills it, or he's gonna know it came from you."

"Okay, okay. I gotta go."

"Fine. Tell the chief I'm out here doing my job."

"You got it."

As soon as Dan was out of sight, Cora headed for her car.

"Hey! Where are you going?" Aaron said.

Cora turned back. "I'm not going anywhere. If Chief Harper asks, I'm around here somewhere, thinking up things to tell Rick Reed."

"But —"

Cora hopped in her car and took off.

CHAPTER 32

The Bakerhaven Police Station was a white frame house with black shutters, just like most other buildings in town. Cora pushed open the front door, went through the outer office, past Chief Harper's office and the interrogation room, and down the hallway to the two small holding cells in the back.

Melvin was in one of the cells. Becky was standing next to it. They were in the midst of a heated argument.

Becky looked around when she came in. "Cora! You shouldn't be here. Get out of here."

"Oh, let her stay," Melvin said. He flashed Cora a smile.

"Melvin!" Becky said irritably.

"We could use a referee. Come in, Cora. We were just having a little discussion about the whole situation. Becky doesn't like my attitude. Can you imagine that?"

"Yeah, well, don't take it personally. She's

not very tolerant."

"That's what I figured. But she's my lawyer. That counts for something."

"Why should it? You're not guilty. It's not like they could hang anything on you."

"My position exactly. But Becky thinks I shouldn't talk because I'm apt to incriminate myself."

"She's just pissed because you took her ten grand."

"Well, why not? It was mine to begin with."

"That's right," Becky said. "Just talk about me as if I weren't even here."

"There's an idea," Cora said. "Why don't you beat it, Becky?"

Becky was incensed. "I'm not going to beat it. Who's the lawyer here?"

"Yeah, beat it, Becky," Melvin said. "I gotta talk to Cora."

Becky's mouth fell open. She gave him such a look. Then she turned and stalked out the door.

"That's not gonna win you any points with the young lady," Cora said.

Melvin shrugged. "Nothing wins me any points with her. She won't go out to dinner. She won't go for a ride. She won't have attorney/client conferences in my motel room."

"What's the matter, Melvin? Getting old? Charm slipping?"

"Hey, I didn't say I was giving up. I just said throwing her out of here probably won't make any difference."

"I'm glad to hear it. What's this all about?"

"Bill French."

"Huh?"

"You never knew Bill French? Funny. Bill French has been a pain in the ass ever since the dawn of time."

"Could you be more specific?"

"Well, you know how I like to gamble? Bill French was a loan shark who stiffed me on the vig."

"How does a loan shark stiff *you* on the vig? You're the one paying it."

"Yeah, if you borrow from him. I didn't borrow from him."

"Then what's this about the vig?"

"Loan shark's gotta get his money somewhere. You ask the loan shark for five grand, if the loan shark ain't got it, the loan shark can't loan it. It happens. A lot of guys into him, nothing coming due. Where's he gonna get the cash?"

"So you loaned it to him?"

"Why not? Who's a better risk than a loan shark? I loaned him five grand."

"What happened?"

"Four hours later he pays it back."

"What's wrong with that?"

"No vig. Where's my five hundred bucks?"

"He didn't pay?"

"Hell, no. He says, oh no, it turns out he didn't need the loan, here's the money back. I don't care if he didn't *need* the loan, the fact is he *took* the loan. And now he's *repaying* the loan, and where's my five hundred bucks?"

"He wouldn't give it to you?"

"No, he gave it to me. He acted like I was sucking his life blood, but he gave it to me." Melvin's face hardened. "Then things started happening. I started hearing whispers. Like how *I* was a bad risk."

"That wouldn't hurt unless you were borrowing."

"Yeah, but it's not the type of reputation you want to have in Vegas. Anyway, that was just the beginning. It happened I was going out with this girl who danced at the Tropicana."

"What a surprise."

"I went to pick her up one night and she's dead."

"What!"

"Yeah. And I can't duck it. Everyone knows I'm dating her. So the police grill me about it, but it's not a suspicious death, and it's no big deal. They let me go and that's the end of it."

"So?"

"So, someone gets an anonymous tip and the next thing you know she's been poisoned, and the cops really do take a dim view of that, so they have a lot more questions, and this time they aren't nearly so nice. The whole thing is a major pain in the ass because I'm married at the time, and they're stupid enough to think that might be a motive."

"Go figure. How'd you get out of it?"

"Well, I had an ironclad alibi. And it turns out the girl was seeing someone else. She was seen with him a couple of times, though no one was able to make an ID."

"Bill French?"

"Had to be. Anyway, every five, ten years, whenever our paths cross, things start to happen. If I work hard enough, I can always trace it back to him. Only this time it went a little too far."

"Are you saying Bill French is the guy in the Dumpster?"

"No. I'm saying Bill French *put* the guy in the Dumpster."

"How do you know?"

"How do I know anything? But I'll bet you a nickel the guy in the Dumpster is a loan shark named Tony di Marco."

"You seen the body?"

"No, but it stands to reason. Because I happen to owe Tony di Marco money."

"You owe the guy in the Dumpster money?"

"Not anymore."

Cora thought that over. "So, Bill French is the guy blackmailing you?"

"No one's blackmailing me."

"You gave Becky Baldwin ten grand."

"Yeah, well, she's cute."

"Don't start with me, Melvin, I'm not in the mood. Are you behind the blackmail or not?"

"I'm not behind anything. I'm being pushed out front and set up. I know who's doing it, but I can't prove it, and I can't do a thing about it."

"Why did you consult Becky Baldwin?" As Melvin started to answer, she added, "Aside from the fact she's cute."

"I had a job I needed done. I didn't want a New York lawyer to do it. I remembered what a good job she did for you."

"There were extenuating circumstances."

"Sure there were. And she used every one of them to her advantage."

"Would this job you wanted done have anything to do with Bill French?"

"I refuse to answer on the grounds that my lawyer is already pissed off at me."

"Melvin."

"Of course I can't help any conclusions you may want to jump to."

"So, you came here to find some legal recourse to stop Bill French. Only buddy Bill wasn't waiting around to be handled. Instead, he started blackmailing you and dropping dead loan sharks you might be associated with in places you might be inclined to frequent."

"I wasn't being blackmailed."

"I know. You're a macho guy. Publish and be damned. Of course, send me to jail and be damned is another story."

"It wasn't like that."

"What was it like?"

"It was like this conversation. Immensely frustrating. You want to get a little closer to the bars?"

"This is not a conjugal visit, Melvin. You're in a holding cell and you haven't even been booked yet."

"You mean that's all it will take? Hell, maybe I'll plead guilty."

"You're incorrigible. All right, who's the dead girl in the cemetery?"

The abrupt change of subject caught him up short. "What dead girl in the cemetery?"

"The one the police think you shot."

Melvin was incredulous. "The police think I shot a girl in the cemetery?"

"Oh, that's right. They only arrested you for discharging a firearm. Well, guess what? The bullet from the firearm they think you discharged hit a girl and she's dead. So why don't you drop the macho routine and let's get Becky back in here and get down to brass tacks."

CHAPTER 33

"All right," Cora said. "So who's the girl in the cemetery?"

"I have no idea," Melvin said.

"Yes, you do. If you're being framed for the guy in the Dumpster, you're being framed for the girl in the cemetery. So who is she?"

"I have to step in here," Becky said. "Anything Melvin tells me is a privileged communication. Anything he says in the presence of a third person is *not* a privileged communication, and the police can inquire into it."

"Yeah," Melvin said, "but they won't know to inquire into it, and I'll lie."

"That's not the point. The point is they can ask *me*."

"And *you'll* lie."

"And put myself in the position of being disbarred."

"Good girl. A lot of lawyers wouldn't

do that."

"I was being sarcastic."

"Hadn't noticed."

"Kids, you can squabble about this later," Cora said. "The fact is, there's another murder charge kicking around, and it won't take long for the police to apply it to you. You were in the cemetery when shots were reported fired. The police responded and picked you up. You were the only one in the cemetery at that time."

"*You* were there."

"Let's not get off on a tangent. No one thinks I did it. Besides, Chief Harper sniffed my gun."

"That's stupid," Melvin said.

"Why? He may not suspect me of killing a girl, but he wouldn't put firing a few shots past me."

"Why would you do that?" Becky said.

"Come on, Becky, snap out of it. I know this case is coming at you from all angles, but use your head. If I stumbled on a dead body and didn't want to report finding it, what better way to get out of it than fire a few shots and let the police investigate? In case they were too dumb to find it, or in case they arrested someone and quit looking, I'd have to come back and help guide them in the right direction."

219

Becky stared at her. "Did you *do* that?"

"Relax. I'm not telling you what happened. I'm telling you why Chief Harper smelled my gun. I didn't fire a shot, so the police are going to think he did."

"No one fired a shot," Melvin said. "I was *there.* There wasn't any shot."

"Yeah, but as your lawyer will tell you, that's a self-serving declaration of no evidentiary value."

"I *would* tell him, except you seem to be running the show. Melvin, she shouldn't be here."

"She's gotta be here. She's the one with all the information."

"Which she's given us. Now she can go."

"I want to hear her theories. They were always interesting. Even when they're way off the mark."

"What's way off the mark?" Cora said.

"Your theory about the hatcheck girl."

"Are you still defending that little tramp?"

"This is not a divorce hearing," Becky said. "I know you've had a colorful past, but we have this present-day murder."

"Two, actually," Cora said. "And the police are going to be looking at him for both. He's going to be asked to identify the bodies. I would suggest you advise him not to lie."

"Why would he lie?" Becky put up her hand. "No, don't tell me with a third party present. Melvin, I've got to hear your story before you say anything else."

"You've heard my story."

"Not in the light of a dead girl by a gravestone. Until you've made a frank and complete explanation to me, I don't want you making it to anyone else. Is that clear?"

"Even Cora?" Melvin said mischievously, stealing a glance at her.

"This is not a *game*," Becky said in exasperation. "This is a case where you could easily go to jail for the rest of your natural life."

"I wouldn't exactly call it natural," Cora said.

The door banged open so hard the walls shook.

Chief Harper strode up to Cora. He was practically apoplectic. "So! I told you to stay at the crime scene! You *agreed* to stay at the crime scene! You told Dan Finley you *were* staying at the crime scene! I come to look for you and what do I get? Aaron Grant stalling me off! You better have a damn good explanation and it better be helpful as hell!"

"I'm sure she does," Becky said. "But she's not going to make it in the presence of my client. *Nothing*'s happening in the presence of my client. My client has no comment on this whole, dreadful situation. Until I've had a chance to confer with my client, which, as you can see, I haven't, as there was no police officer assigned to this station to keep this witness away from my client. So, if you want to talk to Cora, I would suggest your inner office, because we are rather busy here."

Chief Harper looked as if he'd like to shake each and every one of them until their teeth rattled. He controlled himself, managed a tight-lipped smile, and said sweetly to Cora, "After you."

CHAPTER 34

Chief Harper was trying to keep his temper. "You were found at two crime scenes. Most police chiefs, at the very least, would hold you for questioning. But I'm a nice guy, and I'm your friend, and out of the goodness of my heart I let you go."

"You threw me to Rick Reed."

"Big deal. You can run circles around Rick Reed. I bet you didn't tell him a damn thing."

"I don't *know* a damn thing. You shooed me away from the crime scene as soon as I found it."

"Yeah. As soon as you found it. Almost like you knew where to look."

"Thanks for the 'almost', Chief. The only place I knew to look was the cemetery, and that's because of the report of shots fired."

"You didn't know the body was there?"

Cora smiled. "You should listen to my interview with Rick Reed, Chief. He asked

223

the same questions, and I didn't have to lie."

"That's not an answer."

"Not an answer to what?"

"Did you know the body was there before you found it?"

"No, I did not."

Harper studied her face. "Let me rephrase that. I'm not asking if you knew the body was there the first time you found it, I'm asking if you knew the body was there the time you found it when you were searching the cemetery with me."

"I find that question insulting, Chief."

"I find your answer evasive."

"There's nothing evasive about it. I did not know the body was there before I found it with you. Which was the first time I had ever found it. I did not know it was there. Stumbling upon it was a surprise."

Harper shook his head. "I don't like it, Cora. This guy Melvin shows up in town and you start stealing cars and finding dead bodies and I can't even tell if you're lying to me anymore."

"Well, let me set your mind at ease, Chief. I don't know any more about this than you do. Actually, I know a lot less. You find out who the girl was?"

"Not as yet."

"I assume she was shot."

"You can assume anything you like."

"Don't be like that, Chief. I'm not holding out on you, I just don't know much."

"You saw the body. She look shot to you?"

"Well, she didn't look none too good. You pin down the time of death?"

Harper exhaled in exasperation. "Why is it I'm interrogating you, and I'm the one answering all the questions?"

"You're the one with all the info. How can I help you out with this crime if you don't tell me what you know?"

"Help me out with the crime. That's a good one. I don't recall asking you to help me out with this crime."

"You *don't* want me to help you out with this crime? Then what are we talking about?"

Harper bit his lip, tried to remain calm.

"The way I see it," Cora said, "the girl wasn't shot in the cemetery, her body was just dumped there."

"Of course that's how you'd see it."

"Why do you say that?"

"Because Melvin was in the cemetery." Harper shrugged. "Of course, he could have just dumped the body."

"Yeah. After firing the shots that didn't

kill her because she was murdered else-where."

"That's just your theory. I don't have to buy it."

"You do if you don't have a theory of your own."

"I have a theory of my own."

"Oh? What is it?"

Harper said nothing.

"Come on, Chief. How can I ridicule your notions if you won't tell me what they are?"

Harper started to flare up, stopped himself. "Okay, fine. Ridicule my notions. Here's what I figure. I figure Melvin killed the girl in the cemetery. I figure Melvin killed the guy in the Dumpster, too. I figure the murders are tied together. More than likely they were killed with the same gun. If I find out where Melvin hid it, I don't care how good a lawyer Becky is, the guy is history."

"If you find out where Melvin hid it, you're a regular Houdini, Chief, because Melvin didn't hide a gun."

"Maybe Melvin didn't hide it. Maybe he gave it to you."

"You searched my purse. You smelled my gun. It hadn't been fired. Don't you remember, Chief? It wasn't that long ago."

"You mind if I search your purse again?"

"I certainly do. You already searched it, you didn't find anything then, you won't find anything now. Searching my purse is in a legitimate pursuit of your duty. *Repeatedly* searching it smacks of harassment. You could get labeled as a serial purse searcher."

The phone rang. Harper scooped it up, said, "Harper here . . . uh huh . . . uh huh . . . fine, thanks."

Harper hung up the phone and sprang from his desk. "Come with me."

Without holding the door for her, or even waiting for her to follow, Harper strode out of his office and down the hall to the holding cells.

Becky and Melvin had their heads together. She looked up irritably at the chief. "We're not finished."

"Yes, you are," Harper said. "We have a problem. Cora swears she doesn't know where Melvin hid the gun."

"Gun?" Melvin said. "What gun?"

"Hang on, Melvin," Becky said. "He's just trying to goad you into making a statement."

"You're not going to let your client make a statement?"

"I most certainly am not."

"In that case, I have no recourse but to charge him with suspicion of murder."

"And there," Cora said sarcastically, "is a marvelous demonstration of the true meaning of the accused's right to remain silent."

Harper ignored her, kept his eyes on Melvin.

"So," Becky said, "just who is my client charged with killing?"

"The girl in the cemetery."

"Is that how it's going to read at the arraignment? Melvin is charged with killing the girl in the cemetery?"

"Oh, I imagine we'll put a name to her before too long. Toward that end, perhaps you could be of some assistance."

"Excuse me?"

"I'd like to have your client take a look at the body. See if it's anyone he knows."

"I don't need to look at the body," Melvin said. "It's no one I know, it's got nothing to do with me."

"Then I'm sure you'll be eager to establish that fact," Harper said. He took his keys out of his pocket, unlocked the cell.

"Just what do you think you're doing?" Becky said.

"I'm taking the prisoner to look at the girl he's accused of killing."

"Since he doesn't know her, that can't possibly help."

"Or hurt. Anyway, it will be good to

228

establish the fact."

Becky shook her head. "I don't think so."

"That's too bad. That means I'll have to get a court order. It's too late to get one today, which means I'll have to keep him overnight until Judge Hobbs can issue one in the morning. I had hoped to clear this up more judiciously."

"I'm not staying here overnight," Melvin said.

"You are if I say you are," Harper said.

"Becky. Do something."

"There's nothing I can do."

"Cora. Whip out your gun and shoot the son of a bitch."

"Sure, Melvin. But is it okay if I just hold him at gunpoint until you get away? It's hard to live in a town after you shot the sheriff."

"Not going to happen," Harper said. He snapped the handcuff on Melvin's wrist. "I'm going to look at the body. Melvin's arm is coming with me. It would be more convenient if the rest of him followed."

Melvin grinned broadly. "Chief, I like your style. Let's go look at the body, by all means."

"Not a good idea," Becky said.

"It sure beats sitting in a cell. Unless you got a better idea, let's go."

The chief led Melvin outside, put him in the backseat of his cruiser.

"I'm going, too," Becky said.

"Sure you are, but not with him. Least-wise, not back there. You can go with Cora, or ride up front with me."

Becky looked like a little girl who'd been told she couldn't have pie. She slid into the front seat of Harper's car, and slammed the door.

Cora followed Chief Harper to the hospital. She was tempted to pass him and get there first, but figured with the mood the chief was in, that wouldn't be a good idea. She pulled into the hospital parking lot at a moderate speed, caught up with the chief as he, Melvin, and Becky went in the door.

Cora tried to catch Becky's eye in the elevator, but Becky wasn't playing. She caught Melvin's instead. He winked at her. It was all she could do not to roll her eyes.

At the basement level, Becky and Cora stepped out of the elevator and stopped short.

Mopping the hallway was the janitor Cora had hoodwinked into unlocking the morgue for them. If the guy said hi to them, there'd be hell to pay.

There was no help for it. Standing like a statue would be a dead giveaway. Cora

230

nudged Becky in the ribs to get her moving.

At the sight of Cora the janitor's eyes widened. As he opened his mouth to greet her, Cora was running through possible deflections in her head, each one more convoluted and slightly less convincing than the last. Then he saw who was with her — the chief of police and a prisoner in handcuffs — and the janitor was suddenly quite busy mopping the floor. Not that he wasn't watching with interest. He just wasn't initiating any conversations.

Chief Harper marched the prisoner down the hall to the morgue and tried the door. It was locked. He glanced at the janitor. For a moment Cora was afraid he was going to ask the man for the key. That might have led to an embarrassing comment.

The door was pushed open by Dr. Barney Nathan. He must have been in midautopsy. He had a surgical gown on, stained with blood. He frowned. "You didn't tell me it was going to be a convention."

"He's with me," Harper said. "Becky's his lawyer."

Becky had been trying to fade into the background. The doctor's eyes lit up when he saw her. "Ah, Miss Baldwin. How nice to see you again. I'm sorry for the circumstances."

"Don't be. This has nothing to do with my client. As soon as we can establish that, we'll be on our way."

"Of course. Do step in."

Dr. Nathan held the door for Becky, Chief Harper, and the prisoner, and rather grudgingly for Cora. He led them to a slab on the far side of the morgue.

"It's a bit of a mess here. I was just finishing up. But no problem. The face is intact. You should be able to make a good ID."

The sheet over the slab was crimson in the middle. Cora wondered what it was like underneath. Not that she wanted to witness an autopsy firsthand. Still, she was curious. She wondered if Barney was going to whisk the sheet away like a magician performing a grand illusion.

He didn't. He lifted the edges of it gently, pulled it slowly down over her face.

She was attractive. Smooth skin. Blond hair. She looked very much the same under the harsh lights of the morgue as she had under the flashlight at the grave. No marks. No scars. No cuts. Just a beautiful girl, lying on the slab.

Melvin recoiled in horror.

He sucked in his breath, murmured, "Jane!"

CHAPTER 35

"Is he capable of murder?" Harper said.

"No," Cora said. "I'm capable of killing him, but not the other way around."

"I'm serious."

"So am I. Melvin is a big pussycat. Gets by on his charm. His macho posing is an act."

"He taught you how to shoot."

"Sure, he did. But does he carry a gun himself? No. I do, but he doesn't."

"But he knows how."

"He knows a lot of things. It doesn't mean anything. He could probably repair my car, but you wouldn't catch him doing it."

"He knew the victim."

"That's a conclusion on your part."

"He called her Jane."

"So? It's a common name. Hell, it's *her* name. Any unidentified body's a Jane Doe."

"You're just being silly. He knew the victim. And he wouldn't look at the other one."

"Becky wouldn't let him look at the other one."

"Yeah, but the fact is, he didn't do it. What do you want to bet he knows him?"

"If he knows him, it's proof he's being framed."

"Oh, for goodness' sake."

"What's wrong with that?"

"You're like a broken record. You think everyone's out to get your man."

"He's not my man. And people usually are out to get him."

"Why is that?"

"He just generally pisses people off."

"That's the first thing you've said that I agree with."

Becky came in the door. She didn't look happy.

"So," Harper said. "You've had a chance to talk to your client. Are you ready to let him make a statement?"

"Yes and no."

Harper scowled. "Well, which is it, yes or no?"

"I'm not trying to give you a hard time, Chief, but I'm not kicking my client's rights out the door, either. As attorney for Melvin Crabtree, I'm prepared to release a statement in my client's behalf."

"Then you're *not* letting him talk."

"I'm letting him make a statement."

"You're not letting him make it. You're making a sanitized version of it for him."

"I'm glad you understand the situation. My client believes that he is being framed. My client believes the dead girl may be a woman that he was dating. If so, my client believes that she was killed and the killer held onto her body and planted it in a place where he would be found."

"How did the killer know he'd be in the cemetery?"

"There are two possibilities," Becky said. "One, the killer was following him to see where he'd go. When he went in the cemetery it seemed like a good choice. Two, the killer lured him into the cemetery because that's where he'd planted the body."

"Lured him how?"

"That, I couldn't say. These are just possibilities."

"I don't want possibilities. I want facts."

"Of course you do. And we'd love to give you some. Unfortunately, we're not masterminding events, so we don't have them."

"The girl."

"What about her?"

"What's her name?"

"Jane."

"What's her last name?"

"My client doesn't know."

"Your client was dating her and he doesn't know her name?"

"Assuming she's the girl in question, it's possible my client was dating her casually, but didn't know her well."

"I find that hard to believe."

"I don't," Cora said. "I can remember Melvin being somewhat hazy on my name."

"Great," Harper said. "So, what's the rest of your statement?"

"The rest of it?"

"Yes."

"There's no rest of it, Chief. That's the statement."

Harper blinked incredulously. "But you're not explaining anything."

"Unfortunately, we don't know anything. That's why I'm making the statement for him. You see how beat up he'd get if he tried to make one for himself?"

"If you don't have an explanation, I can't let him go."

"We understand that, Chief. Melvin very reluctantly agrees that there is nothing he could say that would make you let him go. He's in jail awaiting arraignment. At which time I shall attempt to get the case kicked for lack of evidence." Becky sighed. "That is the current situation at the present time."

"You don't sound happy."

"I'm not happy. Under the circumstances I'd rather make no statement at all than such an obviously inadequate one. However, Melvin refuses to follow that advice. If I didn't speak for him, he was going to speak for himself. I don't have to tell you what a frightening prospect that is."

"That must be frustrating, but I'm sure he's not the first defendant to feel that way. It's par for the course."

"Yeah."

"Then why are you so upset?"

Becky took a breath, jerked her thumb at Cora. "He wants to see her."

CHAPTER 36

Cora shook her head deploringly. "Melvin, Melvin, Melvin."

He grinned at her. "I do seem to have stepped in it, haven't I?"

"I'm glad you think it's funny."

"I don't think it's funny. There's just nothing I can do about it."

"What do you mean, there's nothing you can do? You're being framed, you know who's doing it. Why aren't you fighting back?"

"I'm not in a very good position at the moment."

"No, you're not. I would think you'd want to get out of it."

"I do. Toward that end I've hired counsel. The nice thing about it, this is a totally legitimate case. She has to take it seriously."

"You're pleased to be framed for murder because it gives you an in with Becky Baldwin?"

"It also gets me in good with you."

"I beg your pardon?"

"Would you be talking with me if I weren't framed for murder? I don't think so. Throw a guy in jail, and the women come a-calling. It's an aphrodisiac."

Cora's eyes blazed. "Okay. For one thing, I'm here because you asked for me. For another thing, I'm here because I think you've lost your mind. If so, you need help. And I don't mean legal. This is a serious situation. If you're not going to treat it like one, you've lost your grasp on reality."

"I haven't lost my grip on anything. I know exactly what's happening. Becky's making my case. She's going to hem and haw, and eventually strike a deal about letting me ID the guy in the Dumpster. He'll turn out to be the loan shark, I'll be charged with his murder, and we'll begin to get the whole picture."

"You've got the whole picture. You already told me the whole thing. Why aren't you telling the cops?"

"Tell 'em what?"

"Tell 'em what? You know who did it. You know the killer. You know the guy who's framing you. Tell the cops about him. They'll pick him up and sweat him, and maybe we'll get somewhere."

Melvin shook his head emphatically. "No, we won't. All we'll get is deeper and deeper. Bill French is framing me for something I did over twenty years ago. Give him something new, and he'll get really angry."

"So what? He's already framing you for murder. What more can he do to you?"

"I have no idea. That's what's scary. The man's a psychopath. He could kill you for jostling him on the subway. Give him cause, and there's no telling what he'd do."

"You're afraid to say he did it?"

"I'm in jail. A sitting duck. What am I going to do, hire someone to taste my food?"

"No, but it's not like you to do nothing."

"Who's doing nothing? I have a lawyer laboring away to secure my release. I have an ex-wife running around pointing out the folly of suspecting me of anything. Just what is it you'd like me to do?"

"Call a press conference. Get Rick Reed and a TV crew in here and tell him you didn't do it."

"What a novel concept. Man arrested for murder claims — and this is going to knock your socks off — claims he didn't do it. What a unique defense. And how ingenious. If only more killers had thought of it."

"If you're not going to be serious, I don't know how I can help you."

"I find it touching that you want to help me. Though I don't know what you could do. Unless you'd like to come a little closer. Speaking of touching."

Cora snorted. "In your dreams."

CHAPTER 37

Judge Hobbs looked down from the bench. "What do we have here?" he asked. It was a formality. He knew damn well what they had there. He'd been discussing it with his wife over breakfast. She'd heard it from Mrs. Cushman of Cushman's Bakery, who'd heard it from Judy Douglas Knauer, the real estate agent, who'd heard it from librarian Edith Potter, who'd heard it from the horse's mouth, a no less unimpeachable source than Police Chief Dale Harper's wife.

District Attorney Henry Firth was on his feet. "Your Honor, we have here the case of Melvin Crabtree, charged with the murder of Jane Cunningham."

"I understand he was originally arrested on a lesser charge?"

"That's right, Your Honor. He was arrested for trespassing and discharging a weapon within town limits. This was upgraded to murder when it turned out the bullet hit someone."

"I see. And is the defendant represented by counsel?"

Judge Hobbs knew that, too. Unless Becky Baldwin was dating the defendant, there was no other reason for her to be there.

"He is, Your Honor," Becky said.

"I see. I assume you plead not guilty to the charges?"

"Not at all, Your Honor."

Judge Hobbs frowned. "You mean you're pleading guilty?"

"I'm not pleading at all, Your Honor. These charges are completely without merit, and I ask that they be dismissed."

"You'll have a chance to argue that at the trial. This is simply an arraignment."

"I understand, Your Honor. But surely a man can't be arraigned simply on a whim."

"I'm sure that is not the case."

"I'm not, Your Honor. I would be interested in the basis for these charges."

"I'm sure you are. But this is not a probable cause hearing."

"This is not a probable cause hearing because there *is* no probable cause. My client was arrested simply for being in the wrong place at the wrong time. That is understandable. What is not understandable is why when no further evidence was forthcoming the charges were not dropped."

"No further evidence," Henry Firth said sarcastically. "You don't count the finding of a dead body as evidence?"

"Not against my client."

"Except for the fact he happens to know her."

"You know the judge. Would you suggest I could proceed against you for murder by producing the judge's dead body and evidence of your relationship?"

Judge Hobbs's gavel silenced the debate. "No one is producing my dead body, figuratively or otherwise. We are dispensing with hypothetical arguments and proceeding with the arraignment."

"That's a little harsh, Your Honor, considering my client's been cooperating with the police."

"By cooperating with the police," Henry Firth said, "are you referring to your client identifying the body in question, not to mention the body of the other victim?"

"Other victim?" Judge Hobbs said.

"Early this morning," Becky explained, "my client assisted the police in identifying the body of the gentleman found in the Dumpster."

Judge Hobbs's wife had missed this tidbit. He raised his eyebrows. "Your client knew both victims?"

"See?" Becky said. "That is just the type of reaction that makes it hard to get a fair hearing. If he identifies both victims you take it as an indication of guilt. If he failed to identify both victims you'd say he was being uncooperative."

"You can make that argument at another time." Judge Hobbs looked at his calendar. "Let's see. I will set a probable cause hearing for — let's see, I have something tomorrow morning — tomorrow afternoon at two o'clock. Meanwhile, the defendant is hereby arraigned on a charge of murder."

"In which case," Henry Firth said, "in light of the seriousness of the charge, I would ask that the defendant be remanded without bail."

"Oh, for goodness' sake," Becky said. "This is why some degree of evidence should be required. I ask the defendant be released on his own recognizance."

"The defendant doesn't live in Bakerhaven, and is a flight risk, in light of the capital charge."

"I tend to agree with the prosecution," Judge Hobbs said.

"What a surprise," Cora muttered.

"What?" Judge Hobbs snapped.

"I didn't say anything," Becky said.

"Someone did."

Cora, sitting on the aisle just behind the defendant, looked positively angelic.

"Very well," Judge Hobbs said. "The defendant is hereby remanded to county jail until our probable cause hearing tomorrow afternoon at two o'clock."

Melvin strained at his handcuffs. "No!"

Judge Hobbs frowned. "I beg your pardon?"

"You can't do that!"

"Oh, but I can. I'm the judge. Ms. Baldwin, could you please control your client?"

"Yes, Your Honor. Melvin, shut up."

Melvin grabbed her sleeve. "Can't go to county!" he hissed.

"What?"

"I can't go to county. Don't let them put me in county."

"You've just been remanded."

"Make 'em keep me here."

"Your Honor, my client objects to being shunted back and forth to county. If the hearing's tomorrow, why can't he stay in the lockup?"

"We don't have the facilities for permanent holding cells." Judge Hobbs banged the gavel. "Defendant's remanded to custody. Next case."

Melvin just had time to flash a pleading

glance at Cora, before Dan Finley hauled
him away.

CHAPTER 38

"You gotta keep him here, Chief," Cora said.

"Oh, for goodness' sake."

"There's no reason to send him to county just to turn around and schlepp him back."

Chief Harper leaned back in his desk chair. "Actually, there is. We're not set up as a jail."

"You got a cell. What more do you need?"

"I got a three-man police squad. Whaddya want me to do, have Dan Finley stay here round the clock until the case comes up for trial?"

"You kept him here last night."

"Yes, I did, and I don't want to do it again. I want to lock up the police station and go home."

"Fine. You do that. Just don't send Melvin to county."

"What's Melvin got against county?"

"He's afraid he'll get a shiv in the gut."

"Oh, come on."

"No, really. You put him in a prison population, he isn't going to last a day."

"That's a little paranoid."

"That's very paranoid. And for good reason. Melvin's the type of guy who makes enemies. Mortal enemies."

"He has an enemy at county? Tell me who, and we'll split 'em up."

"I don't know. It doesn't matter. If he has an enemy, that's that. If he doesn't, someone could pay to have him whacked. In a prison setting he'll have no way to defend himself. His only chance would be to do something so atrocious he gets thrown in solitary. But he'd be doing it on purpose because he has to. Which is hardly fair, considering how it will look to a jury if he's tried for murder."

Becky Baldwin came in the door. "Okay, here's the deal. Melvin doesn't want to go to county because he's afraid someone will kill him there."

"Yes. Cora was just telling me."

Becky scowled. "She was? How is that? He just told me."

"A pretty obvious deduction," Cora said. "Anyway, the chief says he hasn't got the manpower to let him stay."

"Manpower?" Becky was incensed. "My client's life is at stake, and you're concerned

249

with overtime?"

"It's not a question of overtime. No one's here at night. Would your client want to stay here unattended?"

"Is that what you're offering?"

"No, I was just pointing out —"

"Let me talk to Melvin, see if that's agreeable to him." Becky ducked out the door again.

"Damn it," Harper said. "I didn't offer to let him stay here."

"Well, you should."

Dan Finley poked his head in the door. "What's this about letting Melvin stay?"

"I didn't say that," Harper told him.

"Because I can't do another all-nighter. It's one thing to bring in a prisoner and hold him until morning. I can't do two nights in a row. You'll have to ask Sam. And he's not going to be happy."

"Oh, for goodness' sake," Cora said. She stormed out of the office back to the holding cells where Becky and Melvin were arguing hotly. "Kids, kids, let's not get excited."

"That's easy for you to say," Melvin said. "They're not sending you to your death."

"They're not sending you, either. He hasn't even called for the transfer yet."

"He's going to let me stay?"

"I think so. But he's short staffed. You'd probably have to stay alone."

Melvin jerked his thumb at Becky. "That's what *she* was saying. Are you kidding me? I'd rather be in county. You see the lock on the front door? I could get through it in two minutes. And I'm no pro. Then there's the windows. What are they going to do, close the shutters?"

"What's the matter? Are you afraid the killer's gonna bump you off so you can't talk?"

"Wouldn't you be?"

"Yes, I would. So the way I see it, there's only one thing to do."

"What's that?"

"Talk. Tell everything you know. The killer can't stop you from talking if you've already talked."

"She has a point," Becky said.

Melvin grimaced. "She'd have a point if you were dealing with a sane, rational human being."

"Come on, Melvin, you're not that bad."

"Not *me*, damn it! You always have to make jokes. The point is, the rules of logic don't apply. We're dealing with a psychopath. He's not going to want to kill me to keep me from talking. He's going to want to kill me just for the fun of it."

"I see your problem. I can't solve it. The best I can tell you is to try to talk Harper into keeping you here. The police station will be open all day. If worse comes to worst, get someone like me to sit in the outer office with a gun in my purse."

"You'd do that?"

"Not a chance. I got my niece in the hospital with a newborn in intensive care. I don't know if they're going home anytime soon, but when they do, I'm gonna be there for them. I'm not going to get locked into trying to clean up your mess. I'm just saying you should get someone."

Melvin frowned.

Cora grabbed Becky by the arm. "Come on. While he's thinking that over, let's you and me have a little chat." She raised her voice. "Keep an eye on the prisoner, Chief. We're going for a walk."

Becky, who didn't want to make a scene in front of the chief, allowed herself to be wrestled out the door. As soon as they were outside she twisted violently away. "What the hell do you think you're doing?"

"I want to talk to you. Without the help of the police and my dear ex-husband. I want to find out what's going on."

"You know as much as I do."

"No, I don't. I actually know next to nothing. Which is a little weird, since I'm in it up to my eyebrows."

"I don't know what you're talking about."

"Do I have to spell it out for you? This murder is a distraction, but the problem remains. At least, I think it remains. If it doesn't, it will just confirm my theory."

"You're talking crazy, and you're talking in incomplete thoughts. You dragged me out here. What do you want?"

"I'm talking about the blackmail. What did you think I was talking about? I made a blackmail payment. The blackmailer didn't get it because Melvin grabbed the money. If I were the blackmailer, I wouldn't be pleased. I would probably make my displeasure known."

Becky said nothing.

"Did you hear from the blackmailer?"

"No."

Cora nodded. "That's what I thought. And you're not going to hear from the blackmailer, because the person the blackmailer is blackmailing is in jail."

"You're jumping to conclusions."

"Hell, I'm leaping to them. I don't just think Melvin's being blackmailed. I *know* it. And so do you. The killer and the blackmailer are both sending crossword puzzles. Ergo, the killer *is* the blackmailer."

253

Becky frowned.

"The other way I know is you're not trying to get Melvin's money back."

Becky looked at her sharply. "How do you know that?"

"You're not, are you? Which tells the story. Ten grand's not that easy to raise. If you needed it, you'd be trying to get it. So, even if you're cutting me out of the equation, you're not dealing with a blackmail demand."

"What makes you think I'd cut you out of the equation?"

"The same reason you haven't confided in me. Even when the whole deal went south. Anyway, that's why you're not after the money. You don't need it now."

"I see the point."

"Do you? I'm glad to hear it. This is not rocket science. This is a deduction a child of three can make. The reason Chief Harper isn't making it is because he doesn't know about it. The only reason he doesn't know about it is *I'm not telling him.* Because I am a good soldier holding up my end of the bargain. Whereas, everyone else is playing fast and loose with the truth." Cora frowned. "Not me, I mean. I'm playing fast and loose with the police. But within our own conspiratorial circle of no-goodniks,

254

I'm the one being lied to and left in the dark."

"Cora."

"Am I wrong?"

Becky took a breath. "You're wrong about the blackmail."

Cora snorted in disgust.

"I can't talk about the blackmail," Becky said. "As far as the murder goes, you know as much as I do. Melvin is convinced some character from his past is committing these murders solely for the purpose of screwing with his head."

"Bill French."

"Perhaps."

"There's no perhaps about it. That's who it is. Melvin knows it, I know it, you know it. The police don't know it because Melvin won't let you tell them, which is the wrong way to go. You can't hide from a guy like that. The only way to meet him is head-on."

"You can't meet him head-on when you're in jail."

"If you don't try, you're never going to get out of jail. Take my advice. Keep him out of county, get some protection, and tell what you know. You don't want him talking to the cops, go on TV and make a statement."

"That's easy for you to say."

"It's not easy for me to say. If it was my problem, I'd go gunning for the creep myself."

"Why don't you?"

"Oh, there's an idea. Go hunt the bad guy you won't even acknowledge is bad. A fine position that would put me in."

"If you kill him, I'm sure Melvin will talk."

"Now you're just screwing with me," Cora said. "Go reason with your client. See if you can talk some sense into him."

Becky frowned skeptically. "Melvin?"

Cora nodded. "Yeah. Who am I kidding?"

CHAPTER 39

Sherry's eyes were red and her cheeks were caked with tears.

"Easy," Aaron said. "Take it easy."

"Good God, what's happened?" Cora said.

"They won't let me see my baby," Sherry wailed.

"What?"

"They won't let me!" Sherry twisted away from Aaron, sobbed into her pillow.

"Aaron?" Cora said.

"She's running a slight fever. They're afraid of infection."

"The baby has a fever?"

"Sherry," Aaron said. "They won't let her near the baby with a fever."

"Of course not," Cora said. "Sherry. This is perfectly normal."

"This is *not* normal! Normal I'd be holding my baby I would be nursing my baby."

"You will, I promise you. This is just

hospital red tape."

Cora stormed out of the hospital room down to the neonatal ICU. The doctor she'd talked to before was on duty.

"The kid's doing fine. We want to keep her that way. No one sick is going near her. And that includes the mother."

"That's fine in theory, but my niece is distraught. She thinks the kid's at death's door. Nothing you can say is going to help. She thinks it's the end of the world."

The doctor nodded. "Postpartum depression. Not uncommon, particularly after a traumatic delivery."

"If she could just see her baby."

"She'd feel better until the kid came down with pneumonia. That'll send her into a funk she won't snap out of."

"But —"

"Trust me, she'll be fine."

Cora cocked her head. "Remember Shirley MacLaine in *Terms of Endearment* when she wanted the hospital nurses to give her daughter a shot?"

The doctor smiled, shook her head. "Nice try, Miss Felton."

CHAPTER 40

The Channel 8 news van was parked outside the police station.

Cora detoured around it, went inside to find Chief Harper at his desk.

"Melvin's still here?"

"That's right."

"How come?"

Chief Harper leaned back in his chair, sipped his coffee from a paper cup. "He hired a bodyguard. Some New York firm. Guy's on his way up."

"That okay with you?"

Harper shrugged. "What do I care?"

Cora jerked her thumb. "Channel 8's outside. You making a statement?"

Harper shook his head. "Not me. I think Becky is."

"When?"

"She hasn't confided in me."

"Dan can't find out from Rick?"

"I don't really care. She's probably waiting for prime time. Which is silly. If she makes a statement, they'll rerun it all night."

"That's one theory."

"You got another?"

"Sure. She's waiting for the bodyguard to arrive."

"Why? So she can show him on camera?"

"No. She's not looking for publicity." Cora considered. "Come to think of it, that's not a bad idea. But, no, I think she just wants him here."

"Why?"

"In case the statement pisses someone off."

Harper frowned. "I don't think I like that."

"I didn't think you would."

"That's practically implying she has no faith in the police."

"Don't get all macho on me, Chief. You wanna get shot just to prove how tough you are?"

"That's not the point."

"Of course not. Men!" Cora snorted in disgust. "So, you wanna tell me what you've got?"

"You won't confide in me. Why should I confide in you?"

"Well, let's think about that, Chief. Anything you give me, I'm going to give you my opinion. You get a fresh outlook free of

charge. Plus you get to ridicule my theories.
Your own are so bad, it must feel good to
pick on someone else."

"I'm not telling you anything you won't
see on TV."

"I warn you, I have Cinemax."

"What?"

"Come on, Chief. What have you got?"

"The girl can be traced to Melvin."

"No kidding."

"Yeah, but even without his admission. We
found enough friends of hers who can put
'em together."

"On the day of the murder?"

"No, but we can establish the relationship."

"Big deal."

"We can also establish she was cheating
on him."

"I'm shocked."

"It furnishes a motive."

"For what? For not marrying her? For
dumping her and moving on to the next?
Come on, Chief. If Melvin killed every
woman who cheated on him —" Cora broke
off. Her face flushed.

"It's not all we have," Harper said.

"So, what else have you got?"

"We've got a better motive for killing Tony
di Marco."

"That's the guy in the Dumpster?"

"Yes, he is. And Melvin happened to owe him ten thousand dollars."

"Really?"

"Yeah. That figure ring a bell?"

"Why should it?"

"Melvin happened to be carrying that amount of money on him when he was picked up."

"Sure. Wandering around the cemetery in the hope of paying off a dead man. You got any theories that make sense?"

"If he was going to pay off the dead man, and decided to kill him and keep the money."

"Killing a dead man? That's a serious charge, Chief."

"That would leave him with ten thousand dollars, a gun in his hand, and in a rather murderous frame of mind to meet up with the lover who was cheating on him."

Cora shook her head. "All you've got are wild theories, Chief. That's not even enough to go to court."

"I got more than that."

"What is it?"

"I can't tell you."

"Why not?"

"You'll tell Becky."

"No, I won't."

"You're working for her."

"Becky and I are not exactly on the same page. You got something you want me to sit on, fire away."

Chief Harper nodded. He shrugged his shoulders, said almost apologetically, "We got the murder weapon."

CHAPTER 41

Cora was incredulous. "You're sitting on the murder weapon?"

"We're not sitting on it. The prosecutor wants to introduce it in his own way."

"Yeah, by sitting on it."

"He intends to make a statement. He's waiting on the ballistics evidence."

"How long does it take?"

"Okay, he has the ballistics evidence. He's waiting on the news cycle."

"Which is what you think Becky's doing. Which is why you think it's a bad idea."

Harper said nothing.

"Oh, of course," Cora said. "He's waiting her out. Becky's going to make a statement. He's going to let her commit herself before he hits her with the murder weapon."

"And you're not telling her."

"That's hardly fair."

"It was your deal."

"I didn't know this was it."

"Are you going to tell her, yes or no?"

"Where was the murder weapon found?"

"Ah."

"*Ah?* This gets worse and worse. *Ah?*"

"It was in Melvin's car."

"Oh, for Christ's sake!"

"A totally legal search, for which a warrant was duly obtained. We followed all proper procedures."

Cora had some choice comments about warrants, searches, legal and otherwise, as well as the people making searches, the people issuing warrants for said searches, and prosecutors in general and one in particular.

"That's rather unkind to Henry Firth," Harper observed.

"I didn't call him Ratface."

"I think that's the only thing you didn't call him. He's only doing his job." As Cora seemed inclined to donate her opinion of the Bakerhaven prosecutor's job, Harper quickly put up his hand. "You may not like it, but the facts are the facts."

"The facts aren't the facts. The facts are what the killer wants you to believe. Do you really think Melvin's stupid enough to leave the gun in his car? The gun he just fired into a woman? And how the hell did the gun get from the cemetery to his car, can

265

you tell me that?"

"His car was at the cemetery."

That caught Cora up short. It shouldn't have. He had to get there somehow. But she hadn't even thought of it. The case was tying her up in knots. Was she losing it?

Cora took a breath. "His car was at the cemetery. So your theory is he shot her in the cemetery, went back to the car, stashed his gun, then went back and wandered around the cemetery waiting to be caught."

"He killed her in the cemetery. He started to leave. Just before he drove off, he remembered something he forgot. Something crucial. The girl was already dead. He didn't need his gun. He left it in the car, went back to get the incriminating evidence."

"What incriminating evidence?"

"The ten thousand dollars, of course."

Cora looked at him. "The ten thousand dollars he got to pay the dead loan shark, but gave to the dead girl instead?"

"He didn't have to give it to her. Maybe she took it. Maybe that's why he killed her."

"He killed her for the ten grand, but it slipped his mind to take it?" Cora said sarcastically.

"Well, we don't have all the facts yet."

"I'll say. You got one fact, manufactured by the killer to lead you down the garden

266

path, and you fall for it hook, line, and sinker. You're so happy with it you don't even stop to think of the contradictions."

"What contradictions? You're not offering any contradictions. You're offering theories of you own, which aren't any better thought out than the ones you're objecting to."

"They aren't any better thought out because I just *heard* the ones I'm objecting to. How long have you been sitting on this?"

"We searched his car this morning."

"Not till this morning?"

"We had to get a warrant. We got him dead to rights. We're not going to blow it on an illegal search."

"That's what you think."

"That's what I know. Everything's done according to the book, and if there's any problem with the evidence, it's not my fault."

"And that's what it comes down to," Cora said disgustedly. "Not whether or not it's legitimate, but who gets the blame."

"If you had my job, that would be a concern."

"If I had your job, I'd kill myself. Chief, how did you get from arresting bad guys to making sure it's not your fault?"

"Gee, it wouldn't have anything to do with the legal system, would it? The fact if I don't, Becky Baldwin will hang me out to dry."

Cora took a breath. "Never mind that. Damn you, I can't believe you did this. Get me to promise not to tell Becky, and then hit me with the murder weapon."

"I had to."

"What do you mean, you had to?"

"The alternative was not to tell you at all. I didn't want to do that. What with your relationship with the suspect." As Cora started to flare up, he added, "Yes, yes, I know, you have no relationship with the suspect. The point is I didn't want to keep it from you. But I have to keep it from Becky. You see what I mean?"

"I see what you mean. I don't appreciate it."

"You don't?"

"No. This is the justice system. It's not supposed to be some game between opposing counsel. But that's what it's degenerated into."

"I admit it's deplorable. You going to screw me over? It's not like you have to sit on the information long. You probably weren't going to see Becky before then."

"No. I should just let her blindly make a statement."

"How can it hurt her? I mean, more than

268

the murder weapon itself will? What's she going to say that will make it worse?"

"I don't know."

"I don't, either. So, that's the story. You going to keep quiet?"

CHAPTER 42

Cora kept quiet. It killed her, but she did.
She didn't go back and see Becky. She
didn't go back and see Melvin. She didn't
even go see if Becky was holed up with
Melvin, though that was a safe bet what
with Channel 8 staking out the police station. Except the stairs up to her office
wasn't nearly as good a place to film —
you'd be shooting in the alley and no one
would know where you were. And if Becky'd
agreed to make a statement, she'd have told
them where she was going to make it. The
front of the police station was the go-to
place. So the Channel 8 news van gave no
indication where Becky actually was, and if
Cora wanted to find her, she could simply
go look. Or call her on her cell phone. Just
because Cora didn't have a cell phone
didn't mean other people didn't. Did she
even have the number? Had she ever called
it before?

Why was everything elusive and frustrating? Why wasn't she thinking straight?

Why was Melvin back?

Cora went home. It was the safest choice. She could get in the least trouble at home. There was nothing at home she could do.

Nonsense. She could use a computer as well as anyone. Not as well as the average nerd, but as well as anyone who had a life.

What a snide thought. Here she was, striking out blindly in frustration. The point was, she knew her way around a computer. She'd Googled promising sounding men she'd met in chat rooms. None had lived up to their promise, but she'd been able to determine that without going on excruciatingly boring dates, without the benefit of alcohol to make them even slightly tolerable.

She sat down at the computer and Googled Bill French.

He didn't Google.

Impossible. Everybody Googled. But not Bill. Not that there weren't a bunch of Bill Frenches, but none of them were the right age to have been loan sharking in Vegas twenty years ago. Of course, Bill French didn't have to be the guy's actual name, but he'd been going by it, and everybody Googled.

It seemed typical that he wouldn't. Here

271

she was, chasing shadows.

Cora sat down and took out the puzzles. If the killer was the blackmailer and was responsible for all the puzzles, perhaps there was a theme. Something she'd missed. Something she was supposed to see.

The first puzzle was the killer. "Your number is in there. The centermost square." What the hell did that mean? The centermost square of the sudoku was eight. What did eight have to do with anything? It didn't, as far as she could see. Which couldn't be right. The numbers suggested by the second and third puzzles meant something, in one case an address, in the other the number of graves.

So what did the number eight mean?

She went through the puzzles, couldn't find a thing.

Great.

Now what?

It was too early for anything to be happening, even so, Cora went in the living room and turned on channel 8. A game show was running. Cora left it on, went back to the office.

She walked past Sherry and Aaron's room. The door was open and clothes were thrown around. Sure they were. They'd left for the hospital in a hurry. And Aaron, being a guy, hadn't straightened up. Well, that was something she could do. Straighten up.

Cora bit her lip. She could not straighten up. The last thing the kids would want would be someone snooping through their things. They'd just have to come back to a messy room.

Though they wouldn't be coming back to a messy room. They'd be moving upstairs with the baby. The only reason they hadn't moved yet was the baby came early. Cora remembered Aaron making the preliminary move, carrying boxes of things upstairs.

Cora went through the back door into the breezeway/mud room that led to the new addition. The poodle darted along happily. He looked about to lift his leg. Cora shooed him outside, and wandered through the new addition.

The spacious kitchen, damned with the description of modern, was not likely to be used. Not with the cramped but home-style kitchen nearby.

The living room was suitable for entertaining. Cora wondered if she'd be asked to host dinner parties. Realized that was just silly.

She went upstairs to the bedrooms. Over her protest, Sherry and Aaron had insisted on giving her the master suite. It was larger than the other bedrooms and had its own private bath. Cora didn't need a large bedroom. In her current marital situation, she didn't even need a large bed.

A furious yipping below indicated that Buddy was ready to come back in.

Cora went down the stairs — and there was another problem with the addition, did she always want to be climbing stairs? — and let the little poodle in. Buddy, who had no problem with duplex living, went up the flight of stairs like Teddy Roosevelt yelling "Charge!" in *Arsenic and Old Lace*. What a great movie. Was the game show still on?

Cora stuck her head through the doorway to the old house. Yes, the lilt of the bouncy game show music was unmistakable.

Cora trudged up the stairs again.

The baby's room had been outfitted with such things as a crib, changing table, bassinet, and rocking chair. That was all well and good, but with the baby coming home prematurely they wouldn't want to leave it alone, even with a baby monitor picking up every sound. They would want to know if it was moving, twitching, wiggling its fingers and toes — did babies do that? Cora wasn't big on babies, but she was big on her niece. She knew Sherry would want to be there. Sherry would probably even sleep in the baby's room. She'd sit in the rocking chair, or drag a mattress in and sleep on the floor.

Nonsense. The baby's room was for when the baby was big enough to be in a room.

Cora checked out the other bedroom. Sure enough, that was where Aaron had started to move in. So the baby would be right next door. Wouldn't that be close enough?

Not the way Sherry was acting. She'd want to be right in the room. Hell, they might have to physically restrain her from climbing into the crib. And Sherry couldn't be sleeping on the floor. Not after abdominal surgery. She needed to stay put. Have Aaron bring the baby to her. Any chance of that working? Not likely.

So what if they brought the crib in there?

And put it where? The room was too small. There'd be no place for the changing table. They'd be climbing over the crib. It simply didn't work.

Cora went back in the baby's room and moved the crib. It wouldn't fit through the door, but with the mattress taken out, the bottom folded up and the sides collapsed into a parallelogram. Cora rolled it out, down the hall, and into the master bedroom.

It fit, with plenty to spare. Cora was able to move the changing table and the small dresser. There was even room for the rocking chair.

So. That was that. If they didn't like it, it was just too bad.

Cora moved everything Aaron had put upstairs into the master suite. She found sheets in the linen closet and made the bed. Buddy thought that was great fun, and helped out by leaping in the middle every time Cora tried to tuck something in.

Finally she got it done. She stepped back, surveyed her handiwork. Well, it was obvious she'd never been employed as a chambermaid. Still, the rumpled result looked homey.

Cora stuck her head down the stairwell. From the living room she could hear the dulcet tones of Rick Reed.

Good. Let it be Becky. Let it take the weight off her shoulders. The dilemma she'd avoided facing by moving furniture around.

Cora did a double step down the stairs. Buddy did his best to trip her, but to no avail. She hurried through the breezeway, reached the living room while Rick was still delivering his lead-in, explaining at great length about the two Bakerhaven murders, and why Channel 8 news was the best if not the only source of information regarding them.

Becky Baldwin stood in the background,

waiting to be interviewed.

Cora flopped down on the couch, heaved a sigh of relief. Buddy hopped up beside her. Cora gave him a pat.

"And now," Rick Reed said triumphantly, "live and in person, here is Melvin Crabtree's criminal attorney, Becky Baldwin."

"You hear that, Buddy?" Cora said. "Live and in person. As opposed to live and being portrayed in this interview by an actress."

Buddy, unimpressed by Cora's wit, scratched his ear.

"Miss Baldwin," Rick said. "Why is your client in custody? Is he guilty?"

Becky smiled. "I'm glad you asked me that, Rick. That's a common mistake people make. In this country a person's innocent until proven guilty. But we tend to forget that. And so he gets arrested, and we say, 'Oh, he got arrested, he must be guilty.' And very often people aren't. That's why we have safeguards in our legal system. So, no, the fact he's in jail has nothing to do with his innocence or guilt. He's in jail because the wheels of justice grind slowly."

"What do you mean by that?" Rick asked, an old standby he fell back on when he had no idea what someone just said.

"The prosecution has nothing on my client. I have challenged them to produce any evidence of his guilt. They can't do it. Tomorrow afternoon, when they can't do it in front of a judge, my client will be free."

"If he's not guilty, why was he arrested?"

Becky shook her head. "Another common misunderstanding. An arrest is not an indication of guilt. It may be the result of many other things. In my client's case, the facts happen to have been deliberately manipulated."

Cora sat up. Finally, Becky was getting to it.

Rick, of course, took a wrong turn. "By the police?"

"No. Not at all. The police are the ones who have been taken in. You see, my client has been carefully framed. He was lured into the cemetery by an ingenious killer who wanted him to be blamed for the murder. The killer left the girl's body by the gravestone, and made an anonymous phone call, reporting shots fired in the cemetery. The police responded and found my client there. They arrested him, even though he had no weapon on him, and no idea the girl was even there."

"That's shocking." Rick tried to appear shocked. "And who did this? Who killed the girl and framed your client?"

"That's what we want the police to find out."

Cora stood up so fast she startled Buddy, who sprang from the couch yipping in protest.

What the hell was that all about? Was Becky toying with him, or had she just missed her cue?

Neither.

To Cora's astonishment, Becky finished up the interview without ever once mentioning Bill French.

CHAPTER 43

The Channel 8 news van was gone and there was no one in front of the police station. Cora sped by, skidded into a turn, rocketed down the alley, and screeched to a stop in front of the pizza parlor. She hopped out, left the door open and the motor running, thundered up the steps to Becky's office, and pounded on the door.

Becky jerked the door open. "What the hell's the matter?"

"I could ask you the same thing."

"Well, don't. I've got work to do."

"I'll say. I just saw you on TV."

"So?"

"Are you nuts? You didn't mention Bill French."

"Of course not."

"But that was the whole point. Melvin hires a bodyguard. As soon as he's sure he's safe, you can make a statement."

"That's what I did."

"You didn't mention Bill French!"

"He didn't want me to."

"But that's the whole point. *Melvin knows who did it.* Without that, you've got, aw, gee, I was framed, just like every other wise-ass punk who ever got arrested."

"It's frustrating, but it doesn't change anything. He's been arrested. He's been denied bail. That's what I'm dealing with here. Contesting the remand and petitioning for bail. That's assuming I don't get the case kicked on probable cause."

"Becky."

"They've got nothing on him. Nothing. Basically, they got him for carrying too much money after dark. If that's a crime, I'll eat it."

"What was he doing in the cemetery?"

"Minding his own damn business! It's not a crime to wander around the cemetery. At least, not the crime he's charged with. Leave him alone, let me get him out of jail."

"You can't do that without bringing in Bill French."

"Oh, yeah? Just watch me."

"Okay. Fine. I understand the situation and I understand how you're playing it. But it isn't going to work."

"Why not?"

"You're going to get kicked in the teeth."

"How?"

"Challenging the prosecutor on probable cause."

"He doesn't have any."

"Yes, he does."

"No, he doesn't. He's got no witness. He's got no evidence. He's got nothing."

"He's got the gun!"

Becky's mouth fell open. "What?"

"He's got the murder weapon. He's going to spring it on you when you ask for probable cause."

"Where'd they find the gun?"

"In Melvin's car."

"They have a warrant?"

"Yeah."

"So they knew this was happening? This went through legal channels?"

"That's right."

"How long have they had it?"

"Since early this morning."

"How do you know?"

"I can't tell you."

"Why not?"

"I was told in confidence."

"By Chief Harper?"

"I can't tell you that."

"I'm defending a client, Cora."

"I know. That's why I can't let you walk into court tomorrow unprepared. You need to know, you just need to pretend you don't know."

"I can't do that."

"What do you mean, you can't do that? Of course you can do that. You don't have to do anything. You just have to act dumb. For a blonde, that shouldn't be hard."

"My client's interests come first. Anything I've got, I gotta use."

"You don't have to use it, you just have to know it. Now you do, so you can take steps tonight to lay the groundwork for tomorrow."

"Like what?"

"Make another statement. Call Rick Reed up and tell him you got an exclusive."

"An exclusive what?"

"Tell him you'll name the killer."

"I can't do that."

"Sure you can. The killer's a guy named Bill French."

"Oh, yeah, like I'm really gonna do that."

"Why not?"

"Are you kidding? He'll sue me for slander. Assuming he doesn't kill me."

"He won't kill you."

"He might sue me."

"He can't sue you. You're telling the truth. Truth is a defense against slander."

"But I can't *prove* he's a killer." Becky

283

broke off, angry with herself. "Why are we *having* this argument? The point is, I'm not doing it because my client doesn't want it done."

"Your client doesn't know Bill French planted the murder gun in his car."

"And you don't know it, either."

"I know *someone* did. I'll bet you a nickel that someone is Bill French. Melvin doesn't know it *happened.* Tell him and he'll change his mind."

"No, he won't."

"You don't know that till you ask him."

"Yes, I do."

"How?"

"We already discussed it."

"I thought you didn't know it."

"I didn't know it. We discussed the possibility. Melvin thought it was extremely likely since the case against him wasn't strong the killer would try to manufacture some evidence. We discussed what evidence. Murder weapon was the number one answer."

"Well then, we won't give Bill French too much credit for thinking of it. But let's give him credit for doing it. Just stand up and say he did."

"Melvin doesn't want —"

"Right, right," Cora said disgustedly.

"Melvin doesn't want. Because Melvin's just a macho little boy who can't stand to have a little girl say another little boy's picking on him. Which is pretty stupid in this case. So, fine. You're not going to mention Bill French, what are you going to do?"

"I'm going into court tomorrow and beat the case on probable cause."

"Not when they bring in the murder weapon."

"At worst, I'll get him out on bail."

Cora snorted. "Trust me. It's worst."

CHAPTER 44

The police station was locked. Cora banged on the front door until it was opened by a middle-aged man in a gray suit with a bulge under his left arm and a scowl on his face. "What do you want?" he growled. He was a stocky man with a crew cut. In a sweat suit he could have passed for a football coach.

"I want to see the prisoner."

"I gotta pat you down."

"In your dreams. I got a gun in my purse. If I were going to shoot him, I'd have done it years ago."

"Ex-wife?"

"Isn't everyone?"

"Good answer."

The bodyguard pushed the door open. "Hey, Melvin, got a woman here says she married you."

"Could you be more specific?"

"For Christ's sake, Melvin. How many women know you're here?"

"That's Cora. Bring her in."

"She says she's got a gun in her purse."

"I'm sure she does."

The bodyguard followed Cora in and stood next to her and slightly behind.

Melvin grinned. "Cora, this is Clyde Curtis of the C.I.A. That's *Curtis* Investigation Agency, but it's still impressive."

"Melvin loves his little joke."

"Clyde and I go way back. He's a good man if you need someone to shoot first and ask questions later."

"That only happened once."

"Right," Cora said. "You're from New York, you're packin' heat, you're gonna keep Melvin from getting whacked in the night."

Clyde nodded. "Good job description."

"Glad you like it. Whaddya say you let me have a little talk with my ex? Stand guard, make sure no one disturbs us."

Clyde looked to Melvin for approval.

"That would be great," Melvin said.

"You want me to take her gun?"

"I'll risk it."

Clyde went out.

As soon as the door was closed, Cora said, "Okay, shut up and listen. Becky just went on TV and made a generic statement that could have been made by an attorney hired to take the case who hadn't talked to you

287

yet. She's going into court tomorrow to try to get the case kicked or get you bail."

"Tell me something I don't know."

"The killer ditched the murder weapon in your car. The cops have it, and the prosecutor's going to spring it on her when she makes her case."

"That's unfortunate."

"You could say that. Shorter, more graphic statements come to mind. Becky's gotta tell the cops what happened."

"We don't know what happened."

"I mean about Bill French."

"What about Bill French? Haven't seen him in years. Haven't heard from him in years. For all I know, he's dead."

"He's not dead. He's alive, he's framing you for murder, he's capable of anything. That's why you hired Chuckles out there to stand guard. I thought the idea was for you to get him in place so you'd be safe to tell what you know."

"No, the idea was to get him in place so I'd live through the night."

"You're not going to talk?"

"No."

"Why not? It's a win-win. You get to tell your side of the story, and when Bill French gets pissed off and comes after you your private dick shoots him dead."

"It's a nice theory."

"What's wrong with it?"

"More than likely the wrong person would wind up dead."

"If you were out of jail you wouldn't feel that way."

"Maybe not, but I'm not."

"And you're not going to get out of jail until you explain. Can you explain the money in the graveyard?"

"I don't know. Can you?"

"How'd you wind up getting blackmailed?"

"Don't start that again."

"It's the only part of this that doesn't make any sense. I mean, hating you enough to frame you I buy. That motive is right in my wheel house. But blackmailing you just doesn't fit."

"If it did, I'm sure you would have."

"So why are you being blackmailed?"

"I'm not being blackmailed."

"You're not the client?"

"Oh, I'm the client. Just not in the blackmail."

"But you gave Becky the blackmail money."

"So?"

"Why did you do that?"

"I'm a nice guy."

"Come on. I've been married to you. You're not a nice guy. You're a selfish opportunist."

"That's a little harsh."

"Once again, I was married to you. That's mild, by any standard. You wouldn't put up ten thousand dollars to save your best friend from the gallows. What did you get out of it?"

"Nothing."

"What did you hope to get out of it?"

"Ah."

"Oh, of course. You were hoping to get into Becky Baldwin's pants. You haven't yet, so you're playing the good guy card. Instead of the lower-than-a-snake's-belly card that is rightfully yours."

"Were you always this good with words, or is it just since you pretended to do puzzles?"

"You're not helping yourself, Melvin."

"You're not helping me, either. You're in here cross-examining me and pressuring me to put my head on a chopping block."

"You want me to stop pressuring you, tell me who's the client."

"Oh, I can't do that."

"Right. You'd lose all your brownie points."

"Yeah." Melvin's eyes were twinkling. "I'd

probably have to come up with another ten grand."

Cora shook her head ruefully. "You do have a peculiar charm."

"Come over here when you say that."

"Fat chance."

"Come on. I'll tell Clyde to guard the door."

"That's not why I'm here, Melvin."

"Why are you here?"

"I'm trying to help you."

"Come closer."

"Will you tell the cops about Bill French?"

"If I do, will you get over here?"

"I'm serious."

"So am I."

"It's not funny, Melvin. You're talking tough because you got a bodyguard. That's fine for now. But after the probable cause hearing, you know they're going to send you to county. What are you going to do then?"

Melvin shrugged. "Becky's a smart girl. She'll think of something."

CHAPTER 45

District Attorney Henry Firth was angry. He hated to be interrupted when he was eating. It was unfair to his wife, who had cooked the food, and deserved to see it eaten. It would get cold, and it wasn't as good cold. Visitors shouldn't knock at suppertime. Or any time, for that matter. If you wanted to see someone, you called first. Henry flung the door open, prepared to bawl the visitor out.

It was Becky Baldwin, dolled up in a slinky little number. She looked positively gorgeous. She smiled at him. "I'm so sorry to disturb you. I just need a minute of your time."

"We're in the middle of dinner."

"Then I'll be brief. We have a probable cause hearing tomorrow."

"Yes, we do. That's when we should be discussing this. Whatever it is."

"I know," Becky said. "But then you

discuss things and they're on the record, and you don't always want them on the record. So I thought I'd give you a chance to say them off the record, so they don't wind up in the press."

"In the press?"

"Henry, who is it?" Mrs. Firth called from the dining room.

"It's all right, dear, I'll only be a minute," he called back. "I'm sorry, we'll have to do this tomorrow."

"Well, that's too bad. I hoped to clear this up tonight. In that case, I'd like to apologize in advance for accusing you of suppressing evidence in open court."

Henry Firth's face darkened into a scowl. "What!?"

"Yes. It's not the type of thing I like to do, but you have to understand I'm protecting a client. So any accusations of misconduct against the prosecutor are all in the spirit of fair play."

"Fair play? Accusing me of misconduct is not fair play. You think you can pull a stunt like that and get away with it, young lady, you're going to find yourself disbarred."

"See, and I don't want that to happen, either. It would be so much better if we came to an understanding."

"There's nothing to understand. If you

293

make trouble, you're going to *be* in trouble. You think you can come in here, throw false accusations around? Try to intimidate me?" He shook his head. "You have a lot to learn about law."

"I know. So when I start calling witnesses to the stand in order to establish just how long you've been withholding the discovery of the murder weapon, it will be good experience for me."

Henry Firth's eyes were wide. "What? That's ridiculous. No one's withholding anything."

"Have the police uncovered the murder weapon?"

He took a breath. "The police have uncovered a gun which may prove to be the murder weapon."

"What makes you think it is?"

"If you must know, it was found in your client's car."

Becky laughed.

"You find that funny?"

"It is, rather. You assume it's the murder weapon because it was found in the car of the man you assume is the killer. Your circular logic is rather amusing."

"It is the murder weapon."

"How do you know?"

"It fired the fatal bullet."

"Really?" Becky grinned. "You have the ballistics evidence? This gets better and better. You not only suppressed the gun, you suppressed it long enough to get it tested. Then you suppressed it until the results of the ballistics test came in. Then you suppressed it even *after* the results of the ballistics test came in. Court's going to be more fun than I thought."

"Now, see here."

"Are you going to lecture me some more? I certainly hope so. I'm learning a lot. Of course, your food's getting cold. Maybe you should tell me this tomorrow in front of the judge."

"Hold on, hold on. There's no reason to get the judge involved."

"That's what *I* thought." Becky smiled. "But then, I've had dinner."

CHAPTER 46

Cora was third in line at the McDonald's drive-thru window. She'd been forth in line when she got on, but the guy in front took forever to place his order. "It's not a debate," Cora grumbled, while the man discussed his order at some length.

Cora hadn't had a decent meal since Sherry'd been in the hospital. She didn't cook herself, so eating at home was out. And she was too antsy to sit still at the Country Kitchen all by herself.

A banging on the window roused her from her thoughts. Cora looked up. It was Chief Harper. He didn't look happy.

Cora rolled down the window. "Hop in, Chief. I'll buy you dinner."

"Get out of the car!"

"What?"

"You heard me. Out!"

"I can't leave my car here. I'm blocking the line."

"Get out of line."

"I'm hungry."

"Me, too. But am I sitting home eating dinner? No, I'm driving all over town looking for the woman who was supposed to be my friend."

The car ahead of Cora moved up.

"There. You got room. Pull out and park over there."

Cora drove the car over to the parking space. She got out fuming, strode up to the chief. "What is it that couldn't keep until I had my Extra Value Meal?"

"I just had a call from Henry Firth."

"How is Ratface?"

"He's steamed. He's absolutely steamed. And you know who he's mad at? He's mad at me. And you know why?"

"I'm sure you're going to tell me."

"Becky Baldwin disturbed *his* dinner. Guess what she said?"

"Chief —"

"I told you that in confidence. Because I thought you should know."

"I told Becky in confidence because I thought she should know. Looks like we both got taken, Chief."

"What do you mean, we? You're not the injured party here. You're the blabbermouth that caused all the trouble."

"That's a rather unkind thing to say, Chief. I mean, am I calling you a blabbermouth for telling me?"

"This is not a joke, Cora. Becky accused Henry of withholding evidence."

"I'm sure Henry wouldn't do that. He must have some reasonable explanation."

"Can you think of a reasonable explanation? The explanation is I didn't get around to it yet. Does that sound reasonable to you?"

"Well, I'm pretty gullible."

"This is important, Cora. I have to work with these people. I have to keep my job. I've got a daughter in college. You know how much that costs these days?"

"No one's going after your job."

"You didn't hear Henry. I thought he was going to pop a blood vessel."

"It's his own damn fault. When he got the ballistics evidence, he should have called Becky. Not wait to spring it on her in court."

"That's not the point. The point is I told you not to tell anyone. And you said you wouldn't. That's the point. The point is how much I can trust you. How much I can depend on your word. The point is whether I have to worry if you're lying to me."

"Come on. You're a police chief and a husband. You haven't learned that women lie to men?"

Chief Harper looked at her for a long moment. "I thought you were my friend."

He got in his car, pulled out of the parking lot on angry, squealing tires, and sped off down the road.

CHAPTER 47

Cora'd had it. No one wanted to listen to her, no one wanted her help, no one told her anything. All she got was abuse. From people too stubborn to listen. Would it have killed Becky to let her in on the play? Of course not. When had she ever let Becky down? Never. Just the opposite. She was always there for her. And here was Becky treating her as if she couldn't be trusted. She would never betray Becky's confidence. It wasn't in her nature. Oh, sure, she'd told Becky what Chief Harper had said. But that was different. No client would suffer because of it. If that were the case, she wouldn't have done it. And this was the way she was treated. It just wasn't fair.

Cora cruised around in her car and wondered where to go. She hadn't wanted to get back in the McDonald's line. It was too humiliating after being pulled out of it by the cops.

It was really frustrating having nothing to do.

What she wanted to do was find Bill French and slap him silly. How could the guy get away with it? How could Melvin *let* him get away with it? She wouldn't, if it were happening to her. She'd take action. Immediate action. Guy thought he was so tough. Well, she had a gun, too. Assuming he still had a gun, now that he'd planted the murder weapon on Melvin. It didn't matter. Armed or not, Cora wouldn't take it from him.

That was no way to live, cowering in fear. For years she'd put up with it from Sherry, but that was different. Sherry was hiding from a spouse who beat her up. Her ex-husband Dennis was an obnoxious, horrible person, who deserved his place in hell, but Cora couldn't shoot him. He wasn't armed. And, even if he was, she couldn't shoot Sherry's husband. It would put a strain on family relations.

But this son of a bitch was something else. He was a cold-blooded killer, who killed, not out of passion, not even for profit, but for the sheer sadistic plea sure of torturing someone else. Bill French was a scourge that needed to be wiped off the face of the earth. If he came after her, she would have no compunction about pulling the trigger. But he wasn't going to. Because no one was going to name him. He was going to remain in hiding and strike from the shadows.

There was one saving grace. At least with Melvin in jail he wouldn't be killing anybody else. Because that would prove Melvin innocent.

Cora had a funny thought. Suppose she killed Bill French, and made it look like one of his murders. Then he'd be dead, and Melvin would be exonerated. Talk about a win-win. But nothing like that was going to happen. Because no one knew Bill French existed. And that was the way he liked it.

Cora drove out to the hospital. It was after visiting hours. Sherry was asleep. Aaron was gone. It was that type of day.

Cora needed to talk to someone who didn't hate her. She drove over to the *Baker-haven Gazette.*

Aaron was in the bullpen working on his computer.

"Hi, Cora. What's up?"

"What you writing?"

He grimaced. "Rehashing the murder case. I'm trying to make it sound new, but it clearly isn't. Strictly page four."

Poor Aaron. Spending so much time in the hospital with Sherry, he'd missed the leads on both murders. Cora felt sorry for him. She wondered if she should tell him about the gun. She'd told everybody else. Probably not a great idea with the mood the chief was in.

"So what's your angle?"

"I don't have one. I'm hoping my editor doesn't notice."

"Wanna have dinner?"

"What?"

"I'm starving. And everyone hates me."

"What are you talking about?"

"Nothing. I just wasn't ready for another case involving Melvin."

"Yeah, that's gotta be hard." Aaron checked his watch. "I got time for a bite if we don't go far."

"Wicker Basket?"

"Sure."

They walked down the street to the little restaurant with the red-and-white checked tablecloths. It was busy, but they got a table in the corner. Cora had a burger and fries. Aaron had a club sandwich.

"Cheer up," Cora told him.

Aaron looked at her. "Huh?"

"You just had a baby. You're not supposed to be depressed."

"I'm tired."

"No, you're not. You're overwhelmed. You

got married, you built a house, you had a kid. It all seemed so idealistic. Suddenly your kid's got problems, your wife's a basket case, you're running yourself ragged, and you can't even do your job. Of course it's a kick in the head. I know how you feel. I've never had a kid, but I've been married. It always seemed wonderful, and then suddenly it wasn't. And it never got better and ended in divorce."

Cora stuck her finger in his face. "That is not happening to you. You are in a situation that will get better. The kid will get better, and Sherry will get better. Hell, as soon as she gets out of that damn, depressing hospital, things will look ten times better."

"I don't mean to be a drag."

"Yeah, but you can't help it. You have to put on a happy face around Sherry all day. At least, you think you do. You really don't. You just have to be there. If you're worried, be worried. She's not dumb. You treat her like a child, she's gonna think something's wrong."

"I know. I'm writing a nothing piece that doesn't matter that no one's going to read, and I can't even do that right. I started the damn thing three times, I deleted it three times. The problem is there's real stories in the same paper. You got Suspect Arrested,

304

you got Suspect Hires Bodyguard. I could use a quote from Becky Baldwin but I'm not going to get it."

"You called her?"

"Yeah. You know what she said? 'Sorry, Aaron.' I mean, you can quote 'No comment,' or you can say 'Couldn't be reached for comment.' But, when reached for comment said, 'Sorry, Aaron'? Try and fit that into a story." Aaron sighed. "I shouldn't bore you with my problems. What's happening with you?"

Cora hesitated a moment. He looked truly miserable. She took a breath. "How'd you like a front-page story?"

CHAPTER 48

Chief Harper plodded down the drive to see if the paper was there yet. If so, it would be in the metal cylinder mounted on the pole under the mailbox. Harper resented the cylinder, preferred the paper thrown in the driveway. That way he could look out the window and tell if it was there. But that required a nonenvironmentally-friendly plastic cover.

Harper reached the mailbox, stuck his hand in the cylinder. Yes, the paper was there. He wondered if it would be a slam, and, if so, how severe. "Police Drag Feet" was mild, routine, nearly acceptable. "Police Withhold Evidence" was a little harder to stomach. "Police Withhold Murder Weapon" was the worst-case scenario. It was also totally unfair, since it was the prosecutor who was withholding the murder weapon. Harper unfolded the newspaper, prayed that wouldn't be the headline.

It wasn't.

PUZZLE LADY NAMES KILLER
By Aaron Grant

In a stunning development, late last night Bakerhaven's own Puzzle Lady, Cora Felton, named the perpetrator of the two latest murders. According to Ms. Felton, the killer is not Melvin Crabtree, who was arrested yesterday afternoon on that charge, but rather a mysterious and shady individual named Bill French, who has dogged Mr. Crabtree for years, making trouble for him whenever possible. It is Ms. Felton's contention that Mr. French manufactured the evidence that led to Mr. Crabtree's arrest.

Some might discount Ms. Felton's story on the grounds that Mr. Crabtree is her ex-husband. It doesn't necessarily follow. Just last year Mr. Crabtree sued his ex-wife for reduction of alimony, in a bitter, contentious courtroom fight. Moreover, Cora Felton, who has been instrumental in aiding the police in solving crimes in the past, has a reputation for getting things right.

If she is right this time, not only is an innocent man in jail, but a dangerous psychopath is loose in Bakerhaven.

And, according to the Puzzle Lady,
that man is Bill French.

CHAPTER 49

Cora Felton was dreaming.

She was all dressed up in her finest evening gown, a stylishly low-cut number a good three sizes smaller than ones she currently wore but which fit her perfectly, and she was cheering wildly as Jennifer Grant, Sherry and Aaron Grant's daughter, was being crowned Miss America. The proud parents were standing by, Aaron clutching his Pulitzer Prize, and Sherry basking in the recognition she deserved for creating the Puzzle Lady column. Cora, happy to give her the credit now that she'd learned a thing or two about crosswords herself, indeed was just coming off her victory in the American Crossword Puzzle Tournament, the first woman to win the national event since Ellen Ripstein, quite an accomplishment, though she was playing it modest, even though her detractors were trying to knock her down, bang, bang, bang, trying to knock the trophy off the mantle, bang, bang, bang, as if smashing the symbol could take the victory away, still they kept trying, bang, bang, bang!

Cora's eyes popped open.

She was in bed, she couldn't do crosswords, and someone was knocking.

Cora cursed the intruder. She lunged to her feet, pulled on a robe, unlocked the front door.

Chief Harper came through it like a linebacker on a blitz.

Cora staggered back, caught her balance, and asked him what he was doing, though not in those words.

Harper waved the rolled-up newspaper in her face. "I don't believe it! I thought last night was bad. I thought it couldn't get any worse."

"It's not so bad."

"Not so bad! How is it not so bad? Tell m*e one way* in which it's not so bad!" Harper unfolded the paper. "Puzzle Lady Names Killer! You claim you know who the murderer is. You claim he's not the man I arrested. The man due in court this afternoon for a probable cause hearing. The man whose lawyer is already threatening the prosecutor with suppression of evidence. You claim he's being framed and you claim you know who's doing it. Aggravating as that is, it's the type of thing that should be fairly easily disproved. Only guess what? You claim the murderer is Bill French. When we go to look for Bill French, do you know what we find? Nothing! He doesn't exist! What a clever ploy. Accuse a man who doesn't exist. Take the pressure off the real defendant, throw a monkey wrench into the system. It's a false accusation, but you were smart enough not to make it to the cops, and a man who doesn't exist isn't going to sue you for libel."

"I think it's slander, Chief, if the reporter is quoting what I said."

Cora shouldn't have said that. Harper looked close to kicking over the coffee table.

"Is there even the slightest bit of truth in anything you said?"

"Absolutely. It's all true."

"What about Bill French?"

"It may not be his real name, what with there being no record and all."

"Gee, what a surprise. So there may *not* be a Bill French."

"Let's not quibble. The guy exists, whatever you want to call him."

"Oh. So now you're claiming Melvin was framed by persons unknown."

"They're known. They may be known by

another name, but they're known."

"Forget the name. Is any part of what you just told me true?"

"It's all true."

"Can you prove it?"

"I hope so."

"How?"

Cora grimaced. "That's the problem."

"Don't mess with me, Cora."

"The guy's in hiding. I'm hoping to lure him out."

"With press releases? Because if you issue another one . . ."

"Are you threatening me, Chief?"

"I'm warning you. Henry Firth is on the warpath. Becky made this a no-limit game. You just made a big bluff. Henry's going to call you on it. And if you can't back it up, he's going to figure out a charge that will stick."

The front door flew open and Becky Baldwin burst in. Cora had never seen her so excited. She made Chief Harper seem calm.

"Are you crazy? Are you out of your goddamn mind?"

"And hello to you, too," Cora said.

Becky grabbed her by the arms, shook her. "Did you hear what Melvin said? Weren't you listening?"

"Chief Harper's here."

"I see him. I don't care. Do you realize what you've done, making a statement like that? People will think it came from Melvin! People will think it came from me!"

"So what?"

"So what? So what? Make me look like a sleazy, two-bit shyster. Advising my client not to talk, and then leaking stuff to the press."

"You wouldn't do that?"

"It's a despicable practice. It's beneath contempt."

"You *would* do that."

"It's not funny, Cora. Never mind what this does to Melvin's hearing. Never mind what this does to his defense. You put the man in danger."

"Oh, come on."

"People will think it came from Melvin. Guess what? Bill French is one of them. You think he's going to like it? I don't. I think he's going to be angry. You know what happens when Bill French gets angry? People die."

"Oh, for God's sake," Harper said. "It's like you orchestrated this. Rehearsed a little scene to play to sell me on the idea of Bill French. Well, if that's the case, it's a very bad idea."

"I'll say it's a bad idea. You've got a sociopath who kills people just for the sake of annoying others. So you poke him with a stick? Melvin's flipping out. Melvin's afraid to go to court. Melvin says he's a sitting duck."

"He's got a bodyguard, for goodness' sake," Harper said.

"The bodyguard's a sitting duck. At least according to Melvin. Melvin's got him so spooked he called for backup."

"You're kidding."

"Not at all. By the time we leave for court he'll have another man in place."

"What can the guy do in broad daylight?" Harper made a face. "Damn it! Now you've got me talking like he exists."

"That's good, Chief. I can use your help."

"What?"

"I have to persuade Judge Hobbs to sanction two armed guards in his courtroom."

"This just gets worse and worse."

"So what are you here for?" Cora asked Becky. "Just to bawl me out?"

"I wish."

"What do you mean by that?"

Becky grimaced. "Melvin wants to see you."

CHAPTER 50

Melvin went Chief Harper and Becky Baldwin one better. Cora hadn't seen him so angry since they were married.

"Are you an idiot?" Melvin cried. "I know you're irresponsible and irrepressible. But I've never known you to be so self-destructive. Even when you were drinking."

"Watch it."

"Oh, surely they know about your drinking. It was famed across the eastern seaboard. You practically supported Johnny Walker."

"I didn't come here to get beat up." Cora turned on her heel.

"Stop right there!" Melvin bellowed. "I told Clyde to shoot you if you tried to leave."

"As if."

"He's a good man. Don't test him on it."

"I'm not going to stand here and be yelled at."

"Sit down. I got a lot to say and I doubt if I can keep calm."

"Can I go?" Becky said.

"No!" Cora and Melvin said together.

"Take a step and you're dead," Cora added. "I want a witness to what this jackass says."

"You live in a small town. You've had a sheltered life. There's been a few murders, but they've been the genteel sort. Not the blood and guts psycho-killer stuff suspense is made of. You put me in danger, fine, I can handle it. But you put yourself in danger."

"I can handle it," Cora said, patting her drawstring purse.

"Oh, you have a gun, why didn't you say so, that makes all the difference in the world," Melvin said ironically. "He'll never hurt you now."

"He's not coming after me."

"What do you mean? You called him out. You named him in the press. He's going to whack you just as a matter of pride."

"Ridiculous."

"Tell him. Anyway, you're not safe. You need protection."

"No, I don't."

"Tell her, Becky."

"You need protection."

"Clyde!" Melvin bellowed.

The bodyguard stuck his head in the door. "Yeah."

"You got another bodyguard? I want someone on Cora."

"I got just the man you need."

"Yeah? Then why isn't he on his way up here?"

"You just told me."

"If he's so good, why isn't he on his way up here for *me?* Who are you pawning me off on?"

"Are you trying to pick a fight?" Cora said.

"Of course I'm trying to pick a fight. I'm cooped up in jail where I can't do anything. I want to fight the whole world."

"On a more practical front," Clyde said, "ma'am, you want a bodyguard?"

"Like hell," Cora said.

"She wants a bodyguard," Melvin said.

"She says she doesn't."

"She doesn't know any better."

"I can't put a man on her against her will."

"Can you put a man on her without her knowledge?"

"Hey, I'm standing right here."

"The woman has a point, Melvin."

"Give her your card."

"Huh?"

"Give her your card. Cora, take Clyde's

317

business card. You get something you can't handle, you call. Who's she gonna get, Clyde?"

"David McDermott."

"He's the bodyguard?"

"Yeah."

"How quick can he be here?"

"An hour fifteen minutes."

"What if it's urgent?"

"Forty-five. If he doesn't get stopped."

"Give her the card."

Clyde gave Cora his business card.

"Okay," Melvin said, "there's the number. You see a car parked down by the road, you call. You see a car following too close, you call. You see a man taking an interest in you, you call."

"Like the only reason a man would have an interest in me is to kill me?" Cora said.

Melvin cocked his head, grinned roguishly. "That's up to you, babe."

CHAPTER 51

Cora was imagining assassins in the shadows, cars parked down by the road. She cursed Melvin for suggesting it. Now she couldn't get the idea out of her head. There were no cars down by the road. She knew it for a fact. She knew it because she'd checked several times. Damn it to hell.

Not that she was about to hire a bodyguard. That thought never crossed her mind. Well, it did, but only to reject it. She probably didn't even have the card.

Cora dug through her drawstring purse. The first thing she found was her gun. Its weight in her hand, as always, was reassuring. She stuck it back in her purse, rummaged around. Had she stuck it in her wallet? No, that would have been too practical. She'd consigned it to the depths of her purse because she didn't want to find it. She was only looking for it now to pass the time because she'd started getting the creeps.

Cora walked over to the front window, looked out again, saw nothing. She wandered back into the kitchen, continued rummaging in her purse.

She found a pack of cigarettes, pulled it out, lit one. A disgusting habit. She had to quit. If things ever calmed down. Which wasn't likely. Where the hell was that card?

Cora found it, pulled it out. Curtis Investigation Agency. With a Manhattan phone number. The name of the detective she was supposed to call wasn't on it. What the hell was it? Cora couldn't remember. Not that she needed it. She was just spooked. Spooked by a shadow. A man who, as far as Chief Harper was concerned, didn't even exist.

That started a disturbing train of thought. What proof did she have, aside from Melvin's word, that he existed at all? Melvin was a charming liar, had spun elaborate webs in his day. None quite as elaborate as this, but still. He'd never had this motivation. But having to account for two corpses, that was a bit much.

It occurred to Cora she should ask Becky about a paraffin test. That would prove he hadn't fired a gun. Of course, he could have worn gloves. In which case, where would he have disposed of them? They'd have to still be in the cemetery. Could she find them? What was she thinking of? Melvin didn't do that. Bill French did exist.

He might be sneaking up on her right now.

Cora went back to the window. There was still no car down by the street. She took a deep drag on her cigarette, headed back to the kitchen, trailing smoke behind her like a steam engine, her mind going a mile a minute.

If Melvin had made this up, was it possible? Well, let's see. Could he have killed the man in the Dumpster? Easily. Though why he would have done so in that fashion was beyond her. On the plus side, he had a motive to kill him. On the minus side, killing him in that fashion was moronic.

Or was it?

If Melvin was the killer, then Melvin was also the blackmailer, pulling an elaborate blackmail scam on himself. For what purpose? It simply made no sense.

Or did it?

Melvin had a good motive for killing the gambler. And he knew the girl. What motive he might have had for killing her was not yet clear, but say he had one. Then, without the whole blackmail scheme, Melvin stuck out like a sore thumb. Even to her he would look guilty. It was only in the light of the elaborate fiasco in which she found herself, that he too seemed like the victim. And even though he still steadfastly denied being the one being blackmailed, that was just the type of lie he was apt to tell. He could count on her seeing through it, identifying him as the blackmail victim, and thus the victim of a scheme, to lend credibility to the whole Bill French story. More so than if he *claimed* to be the blackmail victim. That would have made her suspicious. No, Melvin being Melvin, he had played it his way, issuing a denial that didn't quite ring true. And how could it? He had to be the blackmail victim, for the simple reason that there wasn't anybody else.

And if he was the victim, then he was also the perpetrator, embroiling himself in a bogus blackmail plot in order to build up his credibility as a man being framed for murder. The only way he could dispose of two people he would likely be accused of murdering without making himself a suspect. At least in her eyes. The police didn't matter. They would suspect him in any case. But if he had her on his side, he could ram his story home. And so the nonexistent Bill French would take the blame. And he had done it so well that she was dodging shadows, afraid of a ghost. The man simply did not exist.

Cora looked out the window, fully expecting to see a car, but there was none. Deciding there was no Bill French did not immediately produce Bill French. No, it merely confirmed her suspicions that her least favorite ex-husband was at it again.

The cigarette burned her fingers. Cora yelped and dropped it. She picked it up gingerly by the filter tip, took it into the kitchen, and threw it in the sink.

The phone rang. A crank phone call? A threatening phone call? Or just someone pissed off at her for the story in the paper? Whatever it was, it couldn't be good.

Cora snatched the receiver off the wall. "Hello?"

"Cora, it's Sherry."

Cora's heart fluttered. The one thing she hadn't thought to fear. What was wrong?

"They're letting me go home," Sherry said. "Can you believe it? They're sending me home."

"Oh, Sherry, how wonderful! So, the baby's all right?"

"The baby's fine. Her lungs are strong enough. She doesn't need an incubator. My fever's down and they're letting me hold her. Can you believe it, I'm actually holding her. I'm holding her right now!"

"That's great."

"So, I'm coming home, and we got a lot of stuff, and I'm afraid to let Aaron drive because he'll keep turning to look at me, you know he will. So, can you pick us up?"

"Of course I can. What time?"

"Two o'clock."

Damn.

Cora never in a million years would let Sherry know, but she didn't want to pick her up at two o'clock. She wanted to be at Melvin's probable cause hearing. There wasn't a prayer Becky would get him out, still she wanted to talk to him after bail was denied. Not that she expected it would make any difference in his story, but still. Would he insist on keeping up the pretense of the two bodyguards?

Well, she could bring Sherry home, get her set up, and rush back to court.

No, she couldn't.

Icy fear gripped her.

If Bill French existed, if one iota of Melvin's story was true, then the most evil, wicked son of a bitch that ever existed would strike at her in any way possible, and what better way than through her niece, the mother of a newborn, the most vulnerable target of all, just home from the hospital, weak, defenseless. She couldn't leave her alone for a moment. Of course, Aaron would be there, and —

Cora's eyes widened.

Good God, Aaron!

His byline was on the story. He was as much a target as she was. Well, not as much, because she had the connection with Melvin, but if Bill French made the connection from her to Sherry to Aaron, and realized he was the one who wrote the story, well, that would be an added incentive. That would be enough to set him off.

Was that a legitimate concern? Of course it was. Damn it, she couldn't just stay home and guard the house.

Cora fished the card out of her purse, picked up the phone, punched in the number.

"Curtis Investigation Agency. This is David McDermott."

Cora recognized the name. "Good. You're the one I want. This is Cora Felton."

"Yes. Clyde said you might be calling. You need a bodyguard?"

"Yes. Well, not a personal bodyguard. I want you to guard the house."

"What do you mean?"

"My niece is coming home from the hospital with a premature baby. I'd like you to protect them."

"Any reason to think they might be in danger?"

"Her husband wrote the newspaper story attacking Bill French."

"He's the danger?"

"That's right. Can you do it?"

"Clyde said to give you whatever you want."

"How soon can you be here?"

"Where's here?"

"Bakerhaven, Connecticut."

"About an hour."

"You need directions?"

"Just the address."

"Hurry."

CHAPTER 52

The nurse at the front desk was adamant. "The emergency room entrance is for emergencies."

"What about discharging patients?"

"That would be the main entrance."

"It's farther from the parking lot."

"Yes. Because discharging patients isn't an emergency."

"Or efficient," Cora muttered. It was already two twenty, and very little progress had been made. Sherry and Aaron were ready to go, but there appeared to be endless paperwork with regard to releasing little Jennifer.

"I beg your pardon?" the desk nurse said.

"Nothing," Cora said.

She stomped off to her car, drove it around directly in front of the main entrance, and went back inside.

"Hey! You can't park there," the desk nurse said.

"I'm not parking," Cora said, without breaking stride. "I'm discharging a patient."

Cora marched across the lobby and up the stairs, so the desk nurse couldn't harangue her while she waited for the elevator. Cora wasn't moving her car for anyone, and it wasn't just that she was fed up with stupid hospital rules. Melvin had gotten her really spooked, and she didn't want to have to be looking for saboteurs while guiding Sherry to the parking lot.

By the time Cora got upstairs, little Jennifer had been sprung from ICU. She looked absolutely adorable in a white knit cap with blue trim. It was too large for her, and kept sliding down over her eyes. Daddy kept adjusting it, but Mama kept batting his hands away.

Sherry was sitting in a wheelchair holding the baby. Aaron was riding herd over her suitcase and a large cloth bag of baby type stuff. Diapers and swaddling clothes, no doubt. Cora wasn't sure what swaddling was, let alone the type of clothes one wore to it.

Cora took her place behind the wheelchair. Aaron picked up the bags.

The baby started convulsing. Milk dribbled out of her mouth.

Sherry screamed.

Aaron dropped everything, ran for help. He came back dragging the ICU doctor, who took the baby out of Sherry's arms with practiced care, and performed the examination right there on the bed.

It was hiccups.

Sherry's heart stopped racing. When she calmed down enough, the doctor gave the baby back.

Cora stood around jabbering nervously and made herself useless while Aaron loaded himself up again.

They went out and rang for the elevator.

Cora wound up pushing the wheelchair, a job she was delighted to be capable of doing. She wheeled Sherry out of the elevator to find the desk nurse and some sort of authority figure waiting to pounce.

"I called security. You have to move your car."

The security guard looked embarrassed at being asked to usher a young mother out of the hospital. He came along and helped them load the car. Cora was thankful for his presence. Not that he would have been any help in case of danger. But his taking over the heavy lifting left her hands free to grip her gun and her eyes free to scan the parking lot. No assassins appeared, and in a matter of minutes Cora was pulling out of the hospital entrance at a greater speed than the situation called for.

"Hey, we got a baby back here," Sherry said.

"I know, it's wonderful," Cora said, swerving onto the road.

"I meant take it easy."

"I know what you meant. I'll be fine."

The ride home didn't take them by the court house, so Cora didn't know if the hearing was still going on. It was one time she wished she had a cell phone. Aaron had one. Should she ask to borrow it? No, Sherry'd hit the roof at the thought of her driving and dialing. She could ask Aaron to call Becky Baldwin. Probably not the most tactful move while bringing home their baby. Cora bit her lip. This was one of the reasons she'd never had children. Not even home from the hospital yet, and already her grandniece was making her behave differently, making her change her lifestyle.

Cora drove home faster than usual, but trying to take it easy on the curves so Sherry wouldn't complain. As she neared the driveway she was on the lookout for any cars, but there were none. That was good in that no one was watching the house, bad in that the bodyguard hadn't shown up.

She got out of the car still on high alert.

She credited Bill French with being fully capable of arriving by taxi, so there would be no car to warn her of his presence. But there was no one there. Besides, Cora figured, if there had been, Buddy would have told her. But he merely charged in circles and peed on a tree.

Aaron helped Sherry inside. That left Cora to carry the baby. She did so with trepidation. Holding a small, living thing was not in her repertoire. And this one was smaller than usual. Cora walked very carefully to keep from tripping, and managed to get the baby through the door of the addition.

The stairs were problematic. Cora and Aaron had to support Sherry on each side to make sure she didn't pull her stitches out. They had a spirited debate over whether they should leave the baby downstairs while they got Sherry up, or bring the baby up first. The Sherry first side prevailed. This was accomplished while the baby resided in a bassinet.

Sherry put up a brief fight about being moved into the master suite, but Cora was having none of it.

"You need the baby in with you and that's all there is to it. You can't believe how happy I will be in the other half of the house."

"You're staying in your old room? You're

not moving into the addition?"

"You're a new mother. You have to get up when your baby cries. I don't. I don't have to *hear* your baby cry."

"You're not moving at all?" Aaron said.

"Maybe when she's older. Like thirty."

Cora left the kids, as she had begun to think of them, upstairs, and went down to the kitchen to call Becky Baldwin. She lit a cigarette to calm her nerves and punched in the number. Wondered how long it would be before smoking was banned in this part of the house.

Becky's answering machine picked up.

Good. They were still in court. Cora hadn't missed it. She could go.

The bodyguard hadn't shown up, but he'd be there any minute. It was pretty far-fetched the killer would go after Sherry and Aaron when the one he really wanted was her. And he was nowhere in sight. Unless he were to materialize magically in the next fifteen minutes, what difference could it possibly make? Absolutely none. She could go.

Cora stayed. Terrified, lest she should make one colossal blunder she would regret for the rest of her life. Even the slimmest chance that such a thing might come to pass, would be to all intents and purposes risking all.

Cora was no coward. She never hesitated to take risks with her own life. But not with Sherry's or Aaron's or Jennifer's — hard to believe something that little had a name. But that tiny thing had become the most precious commodity on earth.

The bodyguard showed up fifteen minutes later, apologizing and blaming a traffic jam on Route 7. An older man, but of reassuringly stocky build, he flashed his shoulder holster and told her not to worry he'd take it from there.

Cora was never so happy to see anyone in her life. She tore out the front door, rocketed down the road.

CHAPTER 53

There was no one at the court house. That was disappointing. She'd missed the whole thing. Cora parked in front of the library and headed for the police station.

Dan Finley came running out.

"Dan. Where are you going?"

"Crime scene."

"What?"

"There's been another one."

"Another what?"

"Murder."

Dan hopped in the car, sped off.

Cora was hopelessly torn. She wanted to talk to Melvin. But she could always talk to Melvin. He was locked up, he wasn't going anywhere.

Cora ran back to her car, pulled out, set off after Dan.

She caught him on the outskirts of town. She fell back and tailed him another mile and a half to a little maple grove on the left.

Three vehicles were parked on the side of the road. One was Chief Harper's. One was Officer Sam Brogan's. One was a black Chevy with New York plates. Sam was stringing a crime scene ribbon around it.

Cora pulled up behind Dan's car. She hopped out and followed Dan.

Chief Harper was standing with his head in the driver's side window of the black Chevy.

"What you got, Chief?" Cora said.

He started, bumped his head. "Damn it. Don't sneak up on a person like that."

Cora stepped in front of him, peered in the window.

A man was slumped over the steering wheel. He was bleeding from a bullet wound in the side of the head. He was a young man, maybe forty-five. Cora grimaced. Had she really started classifying forty-five-year-old men as young?

"Who is it?"

"No ID."

"Is there a puzzle?"

"Don't see one."

"Damn."

"Would you like a puzzle?"

"It would be nice to conclusively tie this murder in with the other two."

"I don't think there's much doubt of that."

"Oh?"

"Bullet wound to the head. Body stripped of ID. It's got the killer's MO all over it."

"I'm surprised to hear you admit that, Chief."

"Why?"

"Are you kidding? It clears Melvin. If he didn't do this one, he didn't do the others."

"Yeah."

Harper was already striding away in the direction of Barney Nathan, who had just driven up.

"Thanks for getting here so fast, Barney. I need a time of death, and I need it now."

"You want it to *be* now, or you want me to give it to you now?"

"Very funny, Barney, but I need it bad."

"Who's the corpse?"

"No ID. Dan's running the plates."

"Can he do that from his car?"

"Huh?"

"Dan's here."

Dan was standing in the background on his cell phone.

"Hell." Harper raised his voice. "Hey, Dan. When you finish tipping off Rick Reed, could you run the damn plate?"

Dan flushed, snapped the phone closed.

Barney Nathan stuck his head through the window, felt the dead man's forehead.

"Warm. I can tell you right now, could have been any time in the last few hours."

"As recent as an hour ago?"

"Hell, as recent as five minutes ago. Unless you were here. But the wound's still seeping. Medically, he could have been just shot."

"I see."

The doctor went back to his work.

Chief Harper turned away.

Cora buttonholed him. "You gotta let Melvin go."

"What?"

"If he didn't do this one, he didn't do any of them. You said it yourself. You gotta let him go."

"Is that how you figure?"

"Come on. You gotta let him go."

Harper shook his head. "I can't let him go."

"Why the hell not?"

"He's not there. Becky Baldwin bailed him out two hours ago."

CHAPTER 54

Cora sped down the road as if the devil were at her heels. Everything was coming apart on her. Everything was upside down and nothing meant what it seemed. The killing that should have exonerated Melvin put him on the hook again. He was out of jail so he could have done it. The police would be picking him up as soon as they knew where he was.

If he was with Becky there'd be nothing to be done, but at least she'd be there to protect him. If he wasn't with Becky, where was he? Well, he'd been in jail for a stretch. When he got out, where was the first place he'd go? Considering there were no houses of ill repute in Bakerhaven, Cora thought wryly. Well, that being true, he'd probably settle for second best.

Cora pulled into the Country Kitchen.

Melvin was seated at the bar. He had a drink in front of him. It clearly was not his first.

The bodyguards sat on either side of him. Neither were drinking. Neither looked happy. They stood up as she approached.

"You'll pardon me, Miss Felton," Clyde said, "but Melvin doesn't want to talk to you."

Melvin waved expansively. "Clyde, Clyde, how rude. You know who this is? This is my wife. Or one of them, anyway. You were my wife, weren't you? This is not some drug-induced hallucination?"

"We need to talk," Cora said. She shot a glance at the bartender. "Not here. How about one of the booths?"

"Sounds romantic. How about it, guys? Think we'll be safe in a booth? You stay here, you can see us just fine, you can see anyone coming from any direction."

Melvin got up from his bar stool, hoisted his drink. "After you, my lady." He bowed and grabbed for her fanny.

"You are sitting on your own side of the table. This is not going to be a wrestling match."

"Killjoy."

Cora got Melvin installed in the booth, sat across from him. "Okay, Melvin. You gotta sober up and focus."

"Pick one."

"Huh?"

"You want me to sober up, or you want me to focus?" He squinted at her. "Where's your bodyguard?"

"I don't have a bodyguard."

"Yes, you do. He called Clyde. Something McDermott. Said you hired him."

"I hired him for Sherry and Aaron."

"That's stupid. You're the one who needs protecting."

"Melvin, I need you to focus."

"I need a drink. How can I focus if I don't have a drink? Clyde!"

"Yeah?"

"Get me a drink."

The bodyguard signaled the bartender. He brought Melvin a scotch on the rocks and withdrew.

"Melvin. Becky got you out of jail."

"Yes, isn't she wonderful? She'd be more wonderful if she'd come out for drinks, but she's still pretty good."

"Get your hand off my knee."

"Did I have my hand on your knee?"

"You know where your hand is."

"Maybe I do, and maybe I don't."

"Melvin!" Cora grabbed his chin. "There's been another murder."

"What?"

"There's been another murder. Just like

340

the other two. It would have been a wonderful break for you if you'd been in jail."

"What the hell are you talking about?"

"A man was found shot dead in his car by the side of the road just outside of town."

"Oh, for Christ's sake."

"Did you kill Bill French?"

"No."

"Did you kill anyone?"

"No. Of course not."

"The police think you did. They're looking for you. I found you first, but they can't be too far behind. Did you kill the man in the car?"

"Don't be silly." He jerked his thumb toward the bar. "These guys have been with me all the time."

"Of course they'd say that. They're in your employ."

"They wouldn't lie to the cops. They got a license."

"If you're paying them, the cops will take their story at less than face value. If the guy in the car turns out to be anyone you know —"

"How could he?"

"I don't know. But the guy in the Dumpster and the girl in the cemetery did."

Melvin rubbed his forehead. "This can't be happening."

"There's no chance the guy in the car is Bill French?"

"He killed himself just to frame me? That would be real dedication."

"No, Melvin, I mean you killed him. You saw it was the only way out. You knew he was never going to stop. You knew how to reach him somehow. The minute you got out of jail you contacted him, you set up a meeting." She jerked her thumb at the bar. "You paid those bozos a ton of money to swear they were here with you. You rushed out, killed Bill French, rushed back here and chugged a few drinks so you could pretend you'd been drinking the whole time. Which is why you were acting drunker than you are."

"It *wasn't* just to seduce you? What did the guy in the car look like?"

"About forty-five. Stocky."

He shook his head. "Too young."

"I could be wrong about that."

"What was his hair like?"

"Brownish, evenly clipped all around."

"Could it have been a wig?"

"Hell, yes. Would that do it?"

Melvin waved it away. "It's not him. Unless you killed him for me. You'd do that, wouldn't you? Just as a favor. To get me out from under. You'd kill him before he killed me."

"In your dreams, Melvin. Okay, tell me this. Did he have anything to do with the blackmail?"

"How the hell should I know?"

"Because you were paying it."

"Let's not go through that again. Yes, I put up the money, no, I wasn't being black-mailed, no, I don't know a damn thing about it, I can't help you there."

"Any chance this guy could be the black-mailer?"

"What guy?"

"The dead guy."

"No."

"How do you know?"

"Because he's dead. I can't speak for when he was alive, but he doesn't seem like much of a threat now."

"Melvin —"

"You wanna know about the blackmail, talk to Becky Baldwin. I just put up the money."

"Where is Becky?"

"She went back to the office."

"I called the office. She wasn't there."

"Maybe she didn't want to talk to you."

"There was no answer."

"You call from your home phone?"

"What?"

"You ever hear of caller ID? If she knew it was you and didn't want to talk, she wouldn't pick up."

"Hell. You got a cell phone?"

"Doesn't everyone?"

"No. Call her, would you?"

"Why?"

"Maybe she'll answer you."

Melvin took out his phone. He punched the number, hit send. "It's busy."

"Damn!"

Cora jumped up and ran out.

CHAPTER 55

"Why don't you answer your phone?"

Becky looked up from her desk. "Oh, were you trying to call?"

"Yes, I was trying to call. Why didn't you pick up the phone?"

"It didn't ring."

"I called. It rang. You didn't pick up."

"If you say so."

"Why didn't you call me?"

"I beg your pardon?"

"To tell me you got Melvin out of jail."

"Oh, I'm sorry. I guess I didn't have my priorities straight. Here I was, bailing him out of jail, and securing his release, and getting his personal items back, and making sure everything was done legal and proper. I should have been calling you instead. I'm very sorry."

"Those personal items happen to include ten thousand dollars?"

"What if they did?"

"Happen to use any part of that for bail?"

"What business is that of yours?"

"If I have to give ten grand to a black-mailer, I'd like to know it wasn't short. But that's not an issue, is it? By now you must have had time to get the money from the real victim and give Melvin his money back." Cora cocked her head. "Unless the blackmail's over."

"Are you talking just to hear yourself talk, because I stopped listening a long time ago."

"You're not concerned about the money. Why is that? Are you going to give it to Melvin? Or are you going to hold onto it in case you need it? What's Melvin buying for ten grand?"

"Damn you!"

"Touch a nerve? Why does *that* touch a nerve? According to Melvin he's getting absolutely nowhere. Of course, it wouldn't be the first fib he's told. But I look at you and I just can't see him denying it."

"Are you quite done?"

"Sorry I missed the hearing. I had to drive Sherry home from the hospital."

"How is Sherry?"

"Sherry's fine." Cora cocked her head, peered at Becky. "Melvin hasn't called you?"

"No one's called me. Unless they called my cell phone. I misplaced it this morning.

I might have voice mail."

"Yeah, you might." Cora studied her face. "I ran into Melvin."

"Where?"

"At the Country Kitchen. Getting drunk."

"I told him to go home."

"That usually does no good."

"I noticed."

Cora sat down, leaned back. "Melvin and I had a nice talk. I put the pieces together and I got some things you should know."

"Do you really?"

"Yeah, I really do. Melvin claims he wasn't being blackmailed. When questioned further, he declines to answer, refers me to you."

"That's not news."

"He tried to call you, but you were on the phone."

"I wasn't on the phone."

"He got a busy signal."

"I haven't been on the phone all day."

"Maybe your receiver's off the hook."

"No, it's fine." Becky picked it up, listened. "Hell."

"What?"

"Line's dead."

"So, you really don't have a phone. Oh, well, don't worry. Melvin's smart enough to keep his mouth shut."

"What do you mean by that?"

"I'm sure he won't say anything until you get there. So there's no rush."

"What?"

"In fact, you could probably just walk around the corner and meet him in front of the police station."

"What the hell are you talking about?"

"When the police bring him in."

"They're not bringing him in. I just got him released."

"Yeah, but they're going to want to talk to him again."

"Oh? Why is that?"

"Someone got killed."

CHAPTER 56

Becky Baldwin was desperately trying to mediate as Chief Harper and Dan Finley led a rather intoxicated Melvin Crabtree into the police station. The bodyguards, who did not look happy, flanked the police officers and watched for saboteurs. Rick Reed filmed gleefully, visions of sound bites dancing in his head.

"I have the right to remain silent!" Melvin announced loudly, slurring his words. "I don't want to exercise that right. I'd like to exercise some other things, but the cops are such killjoys. Speaking of killing, who the hell do they think I killed this time? They won't even tell me. I got two witnesses to the fact I didn't, and here I am being marched off to jail like a common criminal. I am *not* a common criminal. I am a most *uncommon* criminal. As I shall demonstrate, if these stupid cops don't get me killed."

Due to the two bodyguards there was a

bottleneck at the front door. Chief Harper, Becky, and Melvin made it, but Dan Finley got scraped off.

Rick Reed was waiting to pounce. "I am talking with Officer Dan Finley, who just placed the prisoner, Melvin Crabtree, under arrest. Officer Finley, why have you arrested Mr. Crabtree? I thought he was released."

"There's been another murder, Rick."

"So I hear. And you have reason to believe Mr. Crabtree might be involved?"

"I can't say at the present time. But it would seem a reason for revoking bail."

"Come on, Dan, can you help us out here? Who is Mr. Crabtree suspected of killing?"

Dan put up his hand. "Again, we make no allegations at this time. Mr. Crabtree has been picked up for questioning. There was a man shot dead on the outskirts of town, as I believe you have already reported."

"Yes, but it's good to get the confirmation. And who was the victim this time?"

"He has not as yet been identified. We'll let you know as soon as we can."

Dan escaped from Rick Reed's clutches, but not from Cora's. She grabbed him before he could slip in the door.

"Is that true?"

"Is what true?"

"You still haven't identified the corpse?"

350

"I had a problem tracing the plates. Please don't make a big deal about it."

"What problem?"

Dan grimaced. "The chief would be furious at me for telling you. Sam was cranky about being called in — hard to believe, right? So he was less than careful about writing down the plate number. So I don't have the ID yet."

"As soon as you do, let me know."

Dan disappeared into the police station, leaving Cora to hunt for fresh game.

Rick Reed swooped down. "I'm talking to the Puzzle Lady, Miss Cora Felton, who's been so helpful to the police on other occasions. Miss Felton, what do you know about this killing?"

"About as much as you do, Rick."

"Is a puzzle connected to it?"

"What makes you say that?"

"Often, when you're involved, there are."

Rick stopped and his eyes fluttered. Cora could practically see him parsing that sentence, wondering if it made any sense.

"At this time, Rick, we have a stranger killed for no apparent reason. There are no useful clues for me to interpret. When there are, I'm sure you'll hear."

Cora smiled at Rick Reed and glanced around, well aware of how exposed she was on the police station steps in the glare of the Channel 8 spotlight, just in case someone wanted to take a potshot at her. Gunning her down on live TV would be a spectacular stunt. Bill French seemed to have a flare for the dramatic. She wouldn't put anything past him.

Cora scanned the street for potential saboteurs.

Her mouth fell open.

Aaron Grant was in the crowd.

She worked her way over to him, said, "What are you doing here?"

"Covering the arrest."

"Why aren't you home?"

"Sherry made me leave. The bodyguard's more than capable. She and the baby are fine. She sent me to cover the story."

"Who's guarding you?"

"I can take care of myself."

"No, you can't. This is a guy even Melvin's afraid of."

"He's after Melvin, he's not after me."

"You wrote the story."

"You gave me the story."

"I've got a gun. You don't."

"I don't need a gun."

"But —"

"I'll call you if I have any trouble." Aaron

fished in his pocket. "Here, take my cell phone."

"I don't want your cell phone."

"You going home?"

"No."

"Then take the cell phone. I was going to give it to you anyway."

Cora scrunched up her nose. "Why?"

"So Sherry can call you if she needs you. I'm going to the paper to write up the story. She can reach me there. But no one can reach you." Aaron flipped the phone open. "Hell. It's not charged. But it should last the day. Particularly if you're not using it."

"I'm not using it."

"Stick it in your purse. Then Sherry can't blame me for not giving it to you."

"No, just for not charging it." Cora shook her head. "Is the honeymoon over so soon? I thought you guys still liked each other."

"She had a baby. Her hormones are wacky."

"I'll say."

Dan Finley came out the front door of the police station. He saw Cora, put his hands up. "No, I don't have it yet."

"Oh, hell," Cora said. "You got Aaron's cell phone number?"

"Yeah. Why?"

"I got Aaron's cell phone." She held it up,

353

dropped it in her purse. "Call me when you get it."

"Where are you going?"

"Oh, I'll be around."

Cora slipped out of the crowd and took off.

CHAPTER 57

Sherry was happy. She'd just nursed the baby, a triumph in itself. The doctor had warned her Jennifer might be too small to suck hard enough to provide a letdown reflex, but Sherry had no problems on that score. Jennifer had nursed thoroughly and was now sleeping soundly in her crib and everything was right with the world.

Except Aaron. Sherry worried about Aaron. She'd been afraid to let him go, but didn't want to make him stay. She knew he was making allowances and treating her special and changing his life. Yes, the baby was premature, and yes, it would be hard for a while. And yes, Cora did seem to feel there was this crazy shadow hanging over their heads. But for goodness' sake. Some dimly realized figure from her ex-husband's past that even Melvin hadn't seen in over fifteen years. In all probability the killer was not seething with rage because Cora had named him. In all probability the killer was laughing up his sleeve because Cora had no idea what was going on and had named someone else. The idea that the danger attached to Cora and therefore to Aaron the journalist who had written the story was too outlandish to be believed. Aaron was a big boy. He could take care of himself. She'd been right to let him go.

Even so, she wished she hadn't. She wanted him here now with every fiber of her being. If it were up to her, they wouldn't leave the room. They'd lie in bed, watch TV, and order takeout food. Sherry giggled at the thought. Should they put a TV in the bedroom? They hadn't had one downstairs. That was a smaller room, and the living room was right there. Upstairs, with her laid up in bed, things were different.

No, that was silly. She wasn't an invalid. She'd be up and around in days. She'd get the stitches out next week. Heck, she could make it to the bathroom. But could she go up and down stairs? Maybe she should get a TV. If they didn't run the cable they'd only get channel 8. Rick Reed would love that. That was all she wanted. To get live updates from the scene.

That was how Aaron found out about the murder. On the TV in the kitchen. Could she bring that one upstairs? It was a small portable. Could she ask the bodyguard to do it? No, that would be taking advantage. He hadn't been hired to wait on her, just protect her. He was incredibly nice, but she shouldn't take advantage.

Anyway, she didn't need a TV. She could just call Aaron. Her cell phone was in her purse. And where was her purse? She looked around, didn't see it. Remembered. It was on a chair at the bottom of the stairs. She'd set it down to hang onto Cora and Aaron when they helped her up. And with the whole discussion of her and the baby, and who they should bring up first, it had been forgotten. It was still downstairs.

Well, no matter. The phone in the bedroom was installed. Cora'd seen to that. Sherry wondered how many people she'd had to bully, bribe, or threaten to make that happen.

Sherry picked up the receiver.

The line was dead.

Sherry frowned. It had been working before. She'd picked it up to see when she got home. It worked just fine.

Well, it wasn't working now. And, under the circumstances, she really needed the security of a phone.

She'd have to ask the bodyguard. What

was his name? McDermott. Something Mc-
Dermott. Dylan? No, that was the actor.
David. That was it. David.

Sherry called, "David?"

There was no answer.

Sherry craned her neck to listen. From
down the hall she could hear the faint sound
of pop music. Was the bodyguard wearing
earphones? That would certainly seem a
breach of etiquette.

Sherry raised her voice slightly, called,
"David."

Jennifer stirred.

Sherry choked the word back into her
throat.

Damn. Could she get out of bed? She
didn't want to rip the stitches, but how
much of this could she take? It occurred to
her she should have gotten a baby monitor.
It would be ideal for situations like this. She
could keep in touch with the man in the
other room. That wasn't what it was made
for. But surely mothers kept in touch with
nannies, though not necessarily armed ones.

And why was the phone out? It was a new
connection. It shouldn't have failed just like
that.

"David," Sherry called again.

There came the sound of footsteps and
the bodyguard stuck his head in the door.

"Yes, ma'am?"

The bodyguard was balding, but gave the impression he would have had short hair even when it was full. He had that kind of chiseled, rock hard face, the type of man who didn't give an inch, the type of man you wouldn't want to meet in a dark alley, but comforting to have on your side.

"The phone's dead." Sherry felt foolish saying it.

"Here or in the whole house?" He grimaced. "Silly question. How would you know? So, you want to make a call?" He grimaced again. "Another silly question. Why else would you have picked up the phone?"

"I want to call my husband. See if he got to work." She shrugged apologetically. "I know that sounds overprotective. It's just with all these precautions."

"Of course. Don't you have a cell phone?"

"It's in my purse."

"Where's your purse?"

"Downstairs."

"Where?"

"You don't have to get it."

"What else am I doing? Where downstairs?"

"At the foot of the steps. I had to put it down when they helped me up."

"Of course. I'll be right back."

He went out the door.

Well, that was a relief. At least she'd have her phone. And it wasn't just that she wanted to check on Aaron. There'd been another murder. She wanted to know the details. It wasn't idle curiosity. It affected her directly. Another murder would disprove Melvin's theory. Then there was no need for a bodyguard at all. Sherry had had enough tension in the past few days. She didn't need this.

The bodyguard came back with the purse. "Here you go, ma'am. If you want anything, I'll be right outside."

Sherry sat up in bed, snapped open the purse. She reached for the phone, but didn't feel it. She searched the bottom of the purse, but it wasn't there.

Yes, it was. It was there. She knew it was there. She'd checked it on the way home to make sure the battery was charged. And it was. At least three quarters charged. She'd planned to find the adapter, plug it in, charge the phone, once other things were taken care of. But the point is, it was there.

Sherry dumped the purse out on the bed. Squeezed the leather sides. There was nothing in any pouch or pocket. The purse was now empty. It had to be on the bed.

It wasn't.

Sherry pawed through her things, putting them back in the purse one at a time.

No phone.

Jennifer stirred.

Sherry craned her neck, looked.

The baby flailed her arm, didn't wake up.

Sherry heaved a sigh. She couldn't deal with her now.

"David," she called.

There was no answer.

"David!"

Jennifer stirred again.

Sherry sucked in her breath.

The door opened.

The bodyguard started in.

Sherry put her finger to her lips.

He stopped short. Looked over at the baby. Nodded comprehension. He put up his hand, mouthed, "What do you want?"

Sherry motioned him closer.

He came over to the bed.

"I can't find my phone," she whispered.

"Could you have put it down somewhere?"

"I didn't have it."

"When was the last time you saw it?"

"On the way home from the hospital. I checked it in the car."

"Could you have left it there?"

"I put it in my purse." She grimaced apologetically. "I hate to ask you. Could I use your phone?"

"Huh? Oh, sure." He patted his pocket, made a face. "Oh. It's out there. I was making a call. I'll get it."

Sherry put her finger back to her lips.

He tiptoed out.

Sherry looked apprehensively at the baby, but Jennifer was quiet. She realized she'd been holding her breath. This was no good. The irritation, the tension, wasn't good for her. She was supposed to take it easy. A string of unfortunate events had blown that out the window. She needed Aaron after all. She was going to ask him to come back. She hoped he'd finished his story.

The bodyguard came in with the cell phone. "Here you are." He flipped it open. His face fell. "Huh? That's funny."

"What?"

"I left it on. It's off." He pushed the button. Frowned. "It's dead."

"Let me have it," Sherry said. She held out her hand.

"No, I know how to work it. I use it all the time. Something's happened to it." He pressed the button again. "Nothing."

"Gimme," Sherry said.

He handed it to her.

362

She flipped it closed. Flipped it open. Pressed the buttons. Tried various combinations of buttons. Holding them long. Holding them short. She turned it over. Pressed on a sliding panel. It was stuck. She pushed in, pressed harder. A piece slid back.

Sherry sucked in her breath.

"There's no battery."

"What?"

"The battery's gone."

"That's not possible."

"Someone's in the house!" Sherry said.

"No one's in the house."

"The phone is dead. Your battery's missing. My phone is gone."

"It could be coincidence."

"It's not coincidence."

"It doesn't mean someone's in the house."

"Oh, no? Weren't you just on the phone?"

"Yeah."

"Did it have a battery then?"

He frowned. "Huh?"

Sherry blinked. Could he really be that stupid? The man was tough as nails. But not very bright.

He turned. Faced the door. Drew his gun.

"Is anybody here?"

The baby started crying.

CHAPTER 58

Cora almost missed the crime scene. The car had been towed away, but the ribbon was still up, encircling nothing. It was surreal, as if the crime scene itself had been teleported somewhere else.

Cora knew better. She slipped under the crime scene ribbon and began checking the ground.

The police, she knew, had gone over the car with a fine-tooth comb. And they'd found nothing. At least, they hadn't found a puzzle. If they had, Chief Harper would have brought it to her to solve it. If there was a puzzle involved with the third murder it had to be somewhere else.

Of course, it could have been on the body, but in that case Barney Nathan would have found it. True, he hadn't found the one on the first body, but only because it was stuck in the jacket lining. And the killer hadn't done that, Cora had. So by all rights the car and the body were clean.

That left the crime scene. If there was a puzzle, it was here. It was up to her to find it.

The car had been parked far enough off the road to have been in the tall grass and the low bushes. With it gone, it was impossible to tell exactly where it had been. Sam had strung his crime scene ribbon around two stakes and a couple of trees. The tree in front of the car wasn't that near. The crime scene ribbon looked like it had been surrounding one of those super stretch limos the kids used for the senior prom these days, good God, what were parents thinking of? Anyway, that left a lot of ground to cover. It didn't all need covering, Cora just couldn't tell what did and what didn't.

It bugged her that she was looking because Rick Reed had put the idea in her head, asking if there'd been a puzzle with the body. Before he brought it up, it hadn't occurred to her that there might be a puzzle at the crime scene. On the other hand, it hadn't occurred to her that there wouldn't be.

Cora began kicking the tall grass aside with her foot. If the killer left something small enough she had to crawl on her hands and knees to find, the killer was going to get away with it.

Cora had just reached the point where she figured the car couldn't possibly be that long, when she saw it. The corner of a scrap of paper poking out from under a bush.

Could it be that easy? Could the police have overlooked it? Why not? It was garbage. The type of trash that littered the highways. No reason to give it a second look.

Cora reached down, pulled it out.

It wasn't just a scrap. It was a whole sheet of paper.

Cora turned it over.

It was a flier for Walmart.

She was tempted to throw it back. No, she'd be a good girl. She crumpled it up, stuck it in her purse.

That's when she saw it.

A faint movement behind one of the trees in the maple grove.

If she hadn't been hyper alert she would have missed it. But her nerves were raw. She glanced at the tree surreptitiously, while pretending to search a bush.

Had she imagined it?

No, there it was again.

A gray glint behind the maple tree.

The scope of a rifle?

Cora gripped the butt of her gun in her purse, and pretended to scour the ground.

Told herself she was being silly. Could that really be Bill French? The man was diabolical. But to hide out at the crime scene just in the hope that she would come to search it? When the car was gone? And where the hell was *his* car? How did he get here? He walked on foot a good mile just to get the drop on her? Wasn't there an easier way?

To kill her, yes. But to play with her head? This was exactly the right move. Would be having exactly the effect it was having now. Could he have planned that? If so, could she expect a rifle shot from cover? Not killing her, just crippling her, leaving her helpless on the ground so he could walk up and gloat at his cleverness and her folly?

The gray shape moved again. Taking aim?

Then flew up into the branches.

Cora exhaled loudly. Relaxed. Felt like a fool.

The noise was so unexpected she jumped a mile.

Good God! What was that? Had she been shot?

Before she could figure it out, it happened again.

Then she realized. It was Aaron Grant's cell phone.

It was ridiculous how startled she was, but she'd never had a cell phone before.

Where the hell was it?

Oh, yeah. She'd stuck it in her purse.

The phone rang three more times before she managed to find it. She pulled it out, looked at it. Was this one that opened, or one that didn't? It looked like one that opened. There weren't any buttons on it. She turned it sideways, found the groove. Flipped it open.

"Hello?"

"Cora?"

"Yeah?"

"Dan Finley. I thought you weren't going to pick up."

"Yeah, but I did. What is it?"

"I traced the plate."

"And?"

"His name is David McDermott."

And the phone went dead.

CHAPTER 59

Jennifer's wails cut through the night.

He whirled around. "Make her stop!"

Sherry wanted to jump up and run to Jennifer, but had been warned not to. She could rip out her stitches. She could start bleeding internally.

"I can't get up."

"Make her stop."

"Give her to me."

"Okay."

He picked up the baby. Still holding the gun, he cradled her in his arms, rocked her gently. "There there," he said. "There there."

"Give her to me."

"Hush little girl. Hush little girl." He bounced her on his shoulder. The sobs ceased. She started cooing. "There there."

"Give her to me."

He looked at her.

Shook his head.

"No."

"What?"

"No, I don't think so. She's doing well with me. I think I'll hold her a moment."

"Give me my baby."

"Not just yet. You have to make a phone call."

Sherry, overcome, cried, "I haven't got a phone!"

"Yeah." He cradled the baby on one side, dug in his pocket, pulled something out, tossed it on the bed.

Sheer terror gripped Sherry as she tried to catch up with what was going on. She'd been disparaging the bodyguard for being slow, but she was the one whose brain couldn't process. What's happening, what's going on, good God, why won't he give me my baby?

She snatched the thing he threw on the bed. Picked it up and looked.

It was a cell phone battery.

CHAPTER 60

Cora flew down the road hoping a cop would try to stop her. She'd lead them on a merry chase. She wouldn't stop unless they shot her tires. Even then she'd ride the rims. She'd nearly went off the road twice trying to use the cell phone. It was hard to dial a cell phone in a moving car. She'd hardly ever dialed a cell phone anywhere in her life. It wasn't working. Why the hell wasn't it working? She couldn't really look while driving at top speed with one hand.

Cora skidded into a turn, headed for the center of town.

"Be in the street," she said aloud, meaning Dan, or Chief Harper, or any damn cop.

She was the stupidest woman alive, trying to protect her niece by inviting the killer into the house. If anything happened to Sherry, if anything happened to the baby . . .

A man crossing the street leaped out of the way, hurling curses at her tailpipe. But no cops. No help. She was on her own.

Cora set her jaw, floored the accelerator.

CHAPTER 61

A tear ran down Sherry's face.

"Why are you doing this?"

He shrugged. "Because I can. Because I delight in the thought of Melvin seeing it, realizing he caused it, realizing it's all his fault. I'm sure he realizes that by now. He's in the clutches of the law, where I can't get to him. At least, physically. But spiritually. Emotionally. Psychologically. He's mine."

"Give me my baby."

"No, I don't think so." He waggled the gun. "I don't want to shoot a young mother. At least, not yet. Maybe when I'm leaving. But now I just want you not to make trouble. You're not going to make trouble, are you?"

Her lip quivered. "Give me my baby."

He smiled. "See? I don't need the gun." He slipped it back in his shoulder holster. "I have the baby. All I would have to do is drop her. I'm not going to, I'm very sure-handed. I wouldn't drop her. Unless you made me. You're not going to make me, are you?"

"No."

"No. Of course not. As long as I hold the baby, I can make you do anything." His eyes traveled over her. "Anything."

Her flesh crawled. She had to keep from crying out. From doing anything to anger or incite him.

"We have some unfinished business, you and I. We have something I need you to do. You know how to do it. You know where it goes. Stick it in."

Sherry put the battery in the cell phone. Her hands were trembling.

"There you go. Now then, turn it on. The power switch is on the right. See it. You can't miss it. It says power. Press that. Hold."

The cell phone made warm-up sounds.

"There we go. Now, remember. This is not your cell phone. This is my cell phone. There's no one you can reach on speed-dial accidently on purpose. You will have to punch all the numbers in. You know who I want you to call? Not Melvin. He's in jail. Again. Melvin's back in jail again. A cute little refrain. And such a good message. A feel-good song. No, I want you to call his ex-wife. I want you to call your aunt. I want you to call Cora Felton, the Puzzle Lady."

Sherry shook her head, pleadingly. "I can't."

"Yes, you can. You can and you will. Just punch in the number."

"You don't understand. She hasn't got a phone."

"Hmm?"

"She doesn't have a cell phone."

"She does now."

"What?"

"Your husband. The gullible one. The one who wrote that story. Just before he left, I gave him a message. From you. Well, from both of us, really, but I said it was from you. I told him to give her his cell phone. You could get in touch with him through the paper, but we needed to be able to get in touch with her. To call her, you just call him. So go ahead. I'm sure you know the number."

Sherry's breath was coming short. "Please put down the baby."

"Make the call."

"Please."

He held up one finger. "Make . . . the call."

Sherry punched in the number. Held the phone to her ear. Listened. Shuddered. "It went to voice mail."

"What?"

"The phone isn't on. It went straight to voice mail."

"He's a reporter. His phone must be on."

"It isn't."

"I think you dialed the wrong number. Did you do that to me? Did you dial the wrong number?"

"No."

"How can I be sure?" He looked down at the baby.

"No, no, I dialed the right number, I dialed the right number!"

"Let's check on that."

Sherry raised the phone. "Here, I'll show you."

"No, not you. I'll do it."

He reached in his pocket, took out a cell phone.

Sherry gasped.

It was hers.

He flipped it open.

"You must have hubby on the speed-dial, don't you?"

"Yes."

"You wouldn't give me the wrong number, would you? What's his name, Aaron? Let's see. Contacts. Listed under A. Here we are. Aaron. Cell and work. Cell. Enter. Call." He put the phone to his ear. Frowned. "It went to voice mail."

"She doesn't know how to use it," Sherry said. "She probably turned it off by mistake."

"The hell I did. The battery's dead."

He spun around.

Cora Felton stood in the doorway.

She was holding a gun.

CHAPTER 62

"Bill French, I presume? I don't believe we've met. I'm Cora Felton."

He smiled. "Yes. You were running out just as I got here. We didn't have a chance to talk."

"We have time now. Give my niece the baby. Let's have a little chat."

"Melvin taught you to shoot, didn't he?"

"Yes."

"Knowing Melvin, he taught you to shoot first and ask questions later."

"Melvin always was impulsive."

"Yes, he was. If any of that rubbed off, I don't think I'd like it. I think I'll hang onto the baby. Cute kid. I'm getting quite attached to her."

"If you hurt that baby . . ."

"I'm dead. I understand. We have a stalemate here. If I hurt the baby, you'll shoot me. If you shoot me, I'll hurt the baby. It's a no-win situation. So we work it out. I leave, you get the baby back."

"Fine. Put her down."

He grinned. "And trust you to let me walk out? I don't think so. I walk out of here. You don't try to follow, I leave the baby downstairs."

"You take one step toward the door with that baby and I'll blow your head off."

"I didn't think you'd go for that."

"Anyone obsessed enough to carry a grudge this many years, you'd expect them to behave honorably? And for a lousy five hundred bucks."

"Is that what Melvin told you?"

"He said it wasn't the money, it was the principle of the thing. You couldn't stand being stood up to. You wouldn't back down."

"He said it was over money?"

"That's right."

"And you believed him? Melvin?"

"It wasn't over money?" Cora said. She didn't care. She didn't believe him. She just wanted him to keep talking so he wouldn't hurt the baby.

"It was over a girl. Gina. From the Tropicana."

"Yeah. You killed her and framed him for the crime."

"He told you that? It was just the other way around. Gina was his girlfriend. She left him for me. He was furious and he killed her. That's why I hound the son of a bitch. That's why I make his life a living hell."

Cora shuddered. Realized why. It sounded too reasonable. Had Melvin really done that?

Bill French grinned. "So. I'm not such a bad guy. I'm not going to hurt a child. We can work this out."

That snapped her back to reality. Not such a bad guy. Three people dead.

It didn't matter. Keep him talking.

"How'd you know about the bodyguard?"

"Isn't it obvious? I bugged your phone. I bugged the lawyer lady's phone, too. Turned out to be a good move. Not only did I learn you hired the bodyguard, it made it easy to put the phones out of commission."

"How'd you come up with the crossword puzzles?"

"What? Like it's so hard? I thought it was a nice touch, involving his ex-wife. Did the puzzles drive you nuts? Trying to figure out what they meant? The first one was a warm-up. The sudoku. Just for practice. Limber up your brain. But the second one. The one in the Dumpster. I like that. I got a real kick thinking about you solving it. You have any problems with it?"

"Why?"

He chuckled. "Because it can't be solved. Oh, the puzzle can. And the sudoku can. The answer is eight. But what's it mean? That's what drove you nuts."

"So what's it mean?"

"Nothing. It doesn't mean a thing. You could work on it forever and never get anywhere. Pretty neat in itself. But then you got the other two puzzles, and they gave you numbers that *did* mean something. Didn't that make you think again? Didn't you go back and try to figure out what eight meant?"

Cora had done exactly that. She changed the subject, not wanting to give him the satisfaction. "What about the blackmail? What was that all about? Or was that something else that didn't mean anything?"

"No, that was real. You didn't know that? I thought it was obvious. I guess you don't know what to believe anymore. Let me help you out. Call Melvin's lawyer. The blond bimbo. Tell her you're holding the blackmailer at gunpoint and ask her if you should let me get in my car and drive off."

Cora frowned. "What are you saying?"

"I'm saying I'm holding every card in the deck. From the baby. To the photos. To the dope on your ex."

"Photos? What photos?"

"The ones you're paying the ten grand for. Boy was this one sweet caper. The first ten grand doesn't get delivered, so I get to ask for another. And who do you think got the first ten? Go ahead, call her, see what she says."

"I don't care what she says. You're not walking out of here unless you put down that child."

"Here we are again. You know, the thing about this stalemate is, it really isn't. Because you're not going to shoot me while I'm holding the baby. I can go for my gun, and there isn't a thing you can do to stop me."

"Sherry," Cora said. "Sit up straight. Get ready to catch the baby."

"What?"

"I'm going to shoot him in the knee. When he falls forward, catch the kid."

His eyes widened in alarm. His lips started to form the word, "No."

A shot rang out.

His kneecap shattered.

His leg buckled.

He fell, but not toward the bed. Sideways, toward the door.

Cora dived. Flung herself at the floor. Headlong and twisting onto her back.

Reaching out with her left arm. Clutching . . .

Cloth!

Her fingers grabbing the infant, pulling it to her chest, even as she landed on her back, no hands to break her fall, her left hand clutching the baby, her right holding the gun. Wincing in pain from the shock of the fall as she rolled up on her left side just in time to see Bill French reaching in his jacket for his gun.

Cora didn't wait for him to get it.

She shot him in the head.

CHAPTER 63

Downstairs the little poodle was barking hysterically, but miraculously Jennifer was quiet. Sherry picked her up anxiously, but the baby was fine. She cradled and rocked her anyway, just as if she'd been crying, consoling herself as much as the child.

On the floor, Cora was going through Bill French's pockets.

"What are you doing?" Sherry said.

"Nothing," Cora said. She pulled a set of keys out of his pants pocket and stood up. "Absolutely nothing. When the police ask you, remember that."

"Is he dead?"

"I certainly hope so." Cora tossed her gun on the bed. "Here. If he wakes up, shoot him again."

"Cora."

"He's dead. Call the cops."

"Where are you going?"

"Nowhere. Remember that. I didn't go

anywhere."

Cora ran downstairs, where Buddy was still barking hysterically. Bill French had locked him up in the breezeway. She wished she had time to let him out. She flung the door open, dashed outside.

Bill French's car was parked in the drive. Cora ran to it, zapping the doors with his keys as she went. There was nothing in the front seat. Nothing in the back. She opened the trunk. Inside was a suitcase and a briefcase. She unzipped the suitcase, flung it open, fumbled inside. A package stuffed in with the clothes seemed familiar. She pulled it out, opened it. It was full of money.

Cora jammed the package in her purse, zipped the suitcase shut. She opened the briefcase. Inside was a spiral notebook. She flipped through it. The notations seemed to refer to gambling debts or outstanding loans, or something of that nature. Cora couldn't care. She flipped it closed, continued looking.

In a pocket in the top of the briefcase was a manila envelope closed with a clasp. Cora unclasped it, reached in, pulled out the contents. Heaved a sigh of relief. This was it. The blackmail photos.

Cora closed the briefcase, slammed the trunk. She could hear a police siren in the distance. She ran to her car, popped the trunk, threw the package and the envelope inside.

She ran back to the house, took the stairs two at a time, sprinted for the master bedroom, and bent over the corpse of Bill French to shove the keys back in his pocket.

Cora jumped up, grabbed the gun off the bed, and sank to the floor in exhaustion, even as Chief Harper's footsteps thundered up the stairs.

CHAPTER 64

Melvin was contrite. "How can I ever repay you?"

"How about leading a quiet, moral life and never getting into any trouble?"

"Nah, pick something realistic," Melvin said. "How about a nice roll in the hay?"

"How about a nice rap on the head?" Cora said. "You're lucky you didn't get me killed."

"Yeah, right. Like I was the one who told you to accuse the guy in the newspaper. What a great idea. Wonder why I never thought of it."

"You can't hide from a guy like that."

"You can try." Melvin glanced around the front yard. "Nice little house you got here. Which room is yours?"

"It doesn't matter, Melvin. You're not going to see it."

"That's a rather unfriendly attitude. I come up here, no wife whatsoever in tow, hardly even a girlfriend on the horizon."

"You came up here for Becky Baldwin."

"She's not interested. Says I'm old enough to be her father. That's insulting. I'm old enough to be her *grand*father. She's not giving me enough credit."

"My heart bleeds for you."

"So, Bill French is out of my life. Hard to believe."

"Yeah, hard to believe." Cora took a breath. "You know the story he was spreading about you."

"I'm sure there were several."

"The reason he hates you. He said it wasn't about money, it was about the girl."

"Is that right?"

"Yeah. Gina from the Tropicana. Your girlfriend. He stole her away. You were furious and you killed her."

"She was *his* girlfriend. He killed her when he found out she'd been with me."

"I thought that was just to make trouble for you. Because he was angry about the five hundred bucks."

"He was angry about me taking his girl."

"Was there ever any five hundred bucks?"

"Oh, probably."

"Probably?"

"Hell, I don't know."

"You told me this was about the vig on a loan."

"I thought you'd find it more plausible than the jealousy thing."

"Are you kidding?"

"You'd never buy the jealousy thing. Hey, we were always cheating on each other. It was no big deal."

"I wasn't cheating on you."

"What about that blackjack dealer?"

"Are you always going to bring that up?"

"If you're going to start the holier-than-thou routine. I don't care if he's dead. Don't give the son of a bitch the satisfaction of making trouble between us with one last lie."

"Oh, you smooth talker, you."

"Gonna invite me in?"

"It's a crime scene, Melvin. Everybody's back in the old part of the house until the police sort it out. I've got a newborn baby down the hall. That sound like fun?"

"No. That's why we never had kids."

"That and a wide variety of birth control methods. Sometimes overlapping."

"Well, we both knew we shouldn't have kids."

"That's for sure. Hell, your marriages come with an expiration date."

"Let's not spoil things by arguing."

"Particularly when we've had such a good time. Going to jail. Shooting someone."

"Aren't you glad I taught you to shoot?"

"It's my fondest memory of you."

"That's a little harsh."

"Actually, I remember it fondly."

"Me, too. Well, I guess I'll be taking off."

"You going back to the city?"

"Yeah, my business here is done."

"You mean your hot young lawyer wouldn't cooperate."

"Well, she did the work. I just didn't care about the work."

Melvin smiled. He climbed into his car and drove off.

Cora watched him go down the driveway. A man she'd once loved. A man she'd once hated. A man she'd killed for.

She'd done that, hadn't she?

Well, not just for him.

CHAPTER 65

Becky Baldwin pushed the long, blond hair out of her eyes and spread her arms. "Well, it looks like you're in the clear."

"Good to know."

"There's every reason to believe you acted in self-defense. Even though, technically, the man had not actually drawn his gun."

"He was holding a baby."

"That's not considered a deadly weapon in some states."

"I see you got your sense of humor back," Cora said.

"It's so much fun having you as a defendant. Even when you're innocent, you've usually broken several laws."

"Never mind *me.* What about *you?*"

Becky's eyes shifted. "What are you talking about?"

"How'd you get Melvin out of jail? Last I heard, that wasn't even a remote possibility."

"Oh." Becky smiled. "Henry Firth and I cut a deal. I wouldn't raise a stink about him suppressing the discovery of the murder weapon, and he wouldn't contest bail."

"Nice." Cora glanced around the office. She leaned back in her chair, said casually, "It must be a relief now that the blackmail's over."

Once again, Becky had that guarded look. "What do you mean?"

"Well, I think we both agree Bill French was the blackmailer. Kind of goes without saying."

"I suppose."

"Good thing, since Melvin took his money back. I mean, we'd be hard-pressed to make a payment now."

Becky eyed her narrowly. "What's your point?"

Cora reached in her drawstring purse, pulled out the package, tossed it on the desk. "Here's your ten grand. I figured Bill French didn't need it anymore."

Becky's mouth fell open. "You got the money back?"

"I took it out of his car before the police got there. I figured it would only confuse them."

"I'll be damned!"

Cora lit a cigarette. For ten grand, Becky

owed her. "So, Bill French was the blackmailer. Small problem. If the murderer's the blackmailer, how does everything tie together so it makes sense? Well, it doesn't. Unless Melvin's the victim. If he is, it's all part of the same thing. If he's not, it doesn't add up."

Cora blew a smoke ring. "The way I see it, here's what happened. Bill French shows up, starts making trouble. Melvin never sees him, but he knows he's there. He takes precautions. He protects himself physically. And he protects himself legally. He has a reason to consult you, which he's been looking for anyway ever since you first met. He comes up here, hires you as his lawyer, makes a play for you. Bill French sees that, he starts trying to see if he can get something on you. You haven't been practicing law that long, and everything's been above board. As a lawyer, you're squeaky clean. He's gotta go back to college, see if there's anything irregular about your degree. Like a course you should have flunked, if you hadn't been a little too friendly with the professor. He can't find anything like that, but what does he ferret out? Manna from heaven, the fatted calf, the blond bonanza."

Cora threw the manila envelope on the desk. "I took this, too. The blackmail photos.

So you don't have to worry about them anymore."

Becky unclasped the envelope, pulled them out. "Oh, my God!"

Cora shook her head. "I couldn't figure out who your client was. I thought it had to be Melvin, because it couldn't be anybody else. I never knew until Bill French gave me a hint. He told me to call you, ask you if you'd like me to hold the blackmailer for the police, or let him walk away. That's how I knew it was you."

Becky looked up from the envelope, met Cora's eyes. "You have to understand. I was in college. Times were tight. I made money posing for art classes. Someone must have snuck in a camera."

"You don't have to sell me. I just don't understand why you paid off. These are nice photos. But they're not worth ten grand."

"He threatened to put them on the Internet."

"So? If I looked like that, I'd put them on the Internet myself."

"Yeah, and it wouldn't hurt you in the least," Becky said bitterly.

"I'm a young female attorney in a small town. It's hard to get people to take me seriously, particularly looking like I do. I don't want Judge Hobbs seeing this, or

Henry Firth."

"I see your point. I just don't agree."

Cora got up, flicked the cigarette butt out the window. "Anyway, that's how I knew. Bill tipped me off. Bad move on his part. That told me he had to die. I couldn't let him leave, and I couldn't let him blab to the cops. That's something that probably shouldn't come up when you're arguing self-defense."

Becky was incredulous. "Are you saying you shot him dead so he couldn't blackmail me? Or hassle Melvin?"

"Absolutely not. And you can quote me on that. Of course, you won't, because it will never come up. Because I shot Bill French in self-defense. As everyone agrees."

Cora shrugged. "But if you want to think I did, hey, feel free. Like I say, you're young, you haven't got that much experience. You can't tell anyone, but you'll know. And it'll buck you up when you're feeling down and you need a lift. You have a real feather in your cap."

"A feather in my cap? What are you talking about?"

Cora smiled. She felt like the detective in a forties noir movie.

She wished the scene were in black-and-white.

"Hell, you got a killer off," she said, and walked out.

The employees of Thorndike Press hope you have enjoyed this Large Print book. All our Thorndike, Wheeler, and Kennebec Large Print titles are designed for easy reading, and all our books are made to last. Other Thorndike Press Large Print books are available at your library, through selected bookstores, or directly from us.

For information about titles, please call:
   (800) 223-1244

or visit our Web site at:
   http://gale.cengage.com/thorndike

To share your comments, please write:
   Publisher
   Thorndike Press
   10 Water St., Suite 310
   Waterville, ME 04901